Apology For Big Rod

or

The Defiler

Apology For Big Rod

or

The Defiler

by

Charles Holdefer

THE PERMANENT PRESS
SAG HARBOR, NEW YORK

Library of Congress Cataloging-in-Publication Data

Holdefer, Charles.
    Apology for Big Rod / by Charles Holdefer
        p.   cm.
    ISBN 1-877946-93-1
    I. Title
    PS3558.0347746A87   1997
    813'.54--dc20   96-27416
                                      CIP

First edition, October 1997.

THE PERMANENT PRESS
4170 Noyac Road
Sag Harbor, NY 11963

To the Reader

I come to Roderick H. Gass's defense because he is remembered incompletely and spoken of unfairly, even malignantly (you're bastards, some of you: wagging, vicious tongues), which is an injustice I will not let pass, now that my uncle is no longer here to defend himself but is keeping one of the few appointments he ever kept, "*'neath the fine green sod,*" as he used to put it so bluntly, so continentally, "*sucking the roots of dandelions.*"

It is not as a fond niece that I make this plea, but out of respect for his love of life. Whatever his weaknesses or lapses in manners, his jokes without punch lines, he possessed this love: his ability to feel this way and sustain it perhaps unsettles you more than his acts. (Speculation about prison is a cheap shot; Rod had nothing to do with a plot.)

Nowadays, who dares argue the case for happiness? My uncle was contrary enough to do so. The mystery of life didn't faze him: the time he showed it to me he seemed attached to it. *Enough, vicious tongues!*

You know who you are—but nonetheless, to set the record straight, I begin.

"Don't let anyone make you happy against your will."

R.G.

1

How Rod Grew

Uncle Rod was a fragile and sickly infant, according to family reports, a boy the size of a sparrow, grandmother used to say; a boy as smart as a sparrow, grandfather used to say. (Note: this account will flatter no one.) He didn't like to eat, which may come as a surprise to those who knew him later in life when his appetite and its apparent lack of effect on his slim figure was a frequent topic of conversation, as was his gold initialed toothpick, which he carried everywhere and pulled out of his pocket at the end of gigantic Sunday meals to poke his gums with, and if he saw you watching, he'd show you the initials, even offer to let you use it. But in those early years he seemed suspicious of life around him, or at least of the life that was dangled in front of him before he was old enough to choose. There were not only the usual childhood aversions to shoelaces, and to vegetables cooked to a watery mush (still a tradition in our family), but also to nursery sayings like "Rex the Dog," who

In the bog
Ate a pied frog

On a log:
rolled over and died

—or any mention of the idea of heaven. This last left him fearful. A cloudless sky could unnerve him. He had been told that heaven was up there and someday, that

7

was where he'd go, too. For ever and ever. "Up there?" he said, chewing his finger, gazing into the stratosphere. He shook his head, stamped his feet, rattled his untied laces. "No!" Adults found this amusing, and spoke to him of golden streets. Cherubim and heavenly host trailing many wings. His eyes grew bigger. He screamed. According to my father, his little brother cried every day for his first five years—even before he discovered heaven—which made him godawfully disagreeable to be around. My uncle's famous personal magnetism was in no way evident in the early days. Once, during a tense, dim lunch when they were trying to get him to eat a boiled carrot, according to my grandmother, or it was because a breeze had blown up a curtain, exposing a perfect azure sky, a wide-open vault, according to my father, Uncle Rod threw himself violently on the floor, picked himself up, and threw himself down again, picked himself up, and did it a third time before my grandfather could grab him, stop him, and give him a whipping.

"Say you're sorry!"

The hand came down, the cry went up: "*I wish I was never born!*"

He developed into a quiet boy with tender sinuses, fond of insects and throwing a baseball against a barn. He talked to his baseball, named it Carl. My father played with him, of course, but he was older, and interested in different amusements; Uncle Rod learned how to play alone, and actually seemed to prefer it. One day, as a prank, my father wedged a thick stick and left his little brother stranded atop the seesaw. He ran away, abandoned him up there for a long time. (Previously, he'd teased little Rod with angel sightings, fake birthdays, locking him outside in the sunshine—the usual childish penchant for torture.) But that day when my father returned to the seesaw, his brother was unperturbed on his perch, and appeared to have forgotten him. He was talking contentedly to himself. He hollered and hollered when my father let him down. Queerly independent! He was the same about baseball, determined to play on his own, though there was the time my father found him crying under a tree, wetting his mitt with tears and chewing on the laces. When my father asked what was wrong, Uncle Rod looked up with snot on his nose and said that he and Carl had had a fight. (The world was younger then, my father says; my mother, who shares no nostalgia for this side of the family, replies, No, the world was dumber then.) But the next day Uncle Rod and Carl were back together; he was winding up, hurling the ball with a bang! against the barn. In those days there *were* barns, right in the middle of town. Chicago seemed distant; no one anticipated being swallowed up by the city.

At school, Uncle Rod did not distinguish himself. Under his photograph in the 1942 Seymour High Yearbook, they forgot to write anything. But he stayed out of trouble and unlike his later days, stayed out of the newspapers. The photograph of the teenage Rod is disconcerting: his hair is plastered back too far, and there is a startled look in his eyes, as if he is facing not a camera but a gun. His love of life is not yet obvious. Perhaps, at this early juncture, before the flash and wearing a suit that my father says belonged to him, which was too big for his 120 pound brother, held together with pins up and down the back so that it was treacherous to move, even to breathe, Uncle Rod's love of life still needed to break free.

But with the other young men of his class, he graduated from high school and marched off pimply into world war. Everyone agrees, the war changed Uncle Rod. He was never the same after he returned from France. Some say he changed for the worse: if, before the war, he'd never particularly impressed people, at least he'd never offended anyone; Roderick Gass the

9

adolescent claimed no attention for himself. But all you have to do is look at Roderick Gass the man in the Army photograph of '45 to see a transformation: the self-assurance, sweet, dark eyes and trace of a smile, tilted chin, cock of his hat: a *handsome* man, no doubt about it, with a steady fire so conspicuously absent from his yearbook portrait. This Army photo graced my grandmother's mantle for the rest of her life. "Roddy's blossoming," she called it. "Don't he look upstanding, American down to his toes?" Though my grandfather always wondered, "Just what in the hell is he grinnin' about?"

For Uncle Rod had experienced true horrors. He was a passenger in a jeep that struck a land mine, flipped; he was pinned in the mud for twelve hours with a captain whose legs and back were crushed. He watched the man die slowly, a pale, anguished face crying out as he strained to turn around, to touch the limbs that were broken behind him. Sometimes he screamed at Uncle Rod, asked him what he was looking at, why didn't he do something? He ordered my uncle to act. Rod said afterward he wished he could've reached him, if not to help then at least to kill him faster. The man wouldn't stop crying. His face purpled, then drained; violent shivering, staccato grunts. Pain was in no hurry, seemed to have nowhere else to get on to. At one point Uncle Rod forgot the circumstances and thought they were already in a grave, by some terrible mistake. He cursed his misfortune, to have been allotted such a miserable companion! He closed his eyes and shouted, sang to block the man out. Old school songs, radio tunes: "*Yes, dance, hoily boily! Dance! Dance! Dance!*" Yet always there came a moment when he opened his eyes or stopped singing to catch his breath, and there was the man, still crying, shaking, begging God in the mud. Uncle Rod tried again and again to help him but he couldn't move; he watched the agonized face for a while, felt maddeningly neither present nor absent yet

10

inescapably of this clay world. He closed his eyes again to sing. Eventually the man quieted. But his mouth hung open. Uncle Rod, still afraid, sang on hoarsely.

And that was how they heard him. When they pried up the jeep, Uncle Rod crawled out, scrabbling fast, like an insect from under a rock.

His saviors booted him around a little, laughing, then forced him to his feet, took him prisoner. In a makeshift camp outside a village he was put to work salvaging used wire and breaking furniture to be burnt for heat. His diet consisted mainly of potato eyes. One day as he was beating a chair with a stone he felt sick and hungry enough that it dawned on him that he was dying, one more time—his life was indeed a cheap, insect sort of thing—so at extreme risk, he crawled out at dusk and made his escape, with remarkable luck passing through enemy territory and arriving in a village called Tauzé Le Mignon: where, with remarkable misfortune, he was shot through the neck by another American, a man named Albert Livingstone who believed he was from the other side. For this bullet, which passed within millimeters of sure mortality and put him in the hospital for months, he received a letter of profuse apology from Albert Livingstone, and later, a Purple Heart. Uncle Rod returned to Illinois with this letter, his medal, and most conspicuously, a swagger and a lot of morbid talk.

"When I was in the hospital," he revealed, "everybody knew about me. Word got around, they even took pictures. Wasn't nobody more famous on the almost-dead ward than me."

At first people were so pleased to see Uncle Rod come home alive, making a fuss over him and his medal, that they forgave him his swagger (not the style in our family) and even allowed that he might've earned it, after what he'd been through. And as for the morbid talk (which was more than bad manners with us; until now, a sin)—well, in time he'd get over that and speak more reasonably like everyone else. Wouldn't he?

But Uncle Rod didn't change, and acquired a reputation for a swollen head.

"I know what I'm talking about. You might as well kick back and do as you damn please in this world, since the worms are licking at your heels anyway. You hear me?"

If someone tried to improve the conversation by praising him for his Purple Heart, remarking that it must mean a lot to him, he turned the compliment around. He pushed out his lips.

"An intact body and mind are the only hard currency in this world. A Purple Heart, why, that's just a symbol, and when you see a symbol, if you have any sense, you should smell a rat! I'm for straight words."

He started referring to himself by a nickname he'd acquired in the service, Big Rod, which the rest of the family found ridiculous—why, he wasn't big, he was a smallish man with compact muscles. The only thing big about him was his talk. Who did he think he was?

"In the days I got left, folks, you can bet I'm gonna do what I want to do! There's so much more to be!"

He didn't feel like holding a regular job. This, this above all brought a stern judgment down upon his head; no prior exploit could excuse it. For work wasn't just daily bread, though that was nothing to sneer at, at a time when the Seymour City Park saw traveling men sleeping on picnic tables, downstate drifters and ex-farm boys and Mexicans, on their way to or from Chicago. At first, people feared the situation would be as tough as before the war, when the future was thin, thin ice and my grandfather earned ten cents a head for each person he turned in for stealing coal or sleeping under machine sheds at the local railway yard. A deep-rooted conviction held that work was the only shield; work was the glue that held life together. How could Uncle Rod pretend to ignore such a fact? Off and on he sold Fuller Brushes from door to door, when he felt like it; that he managed to make any money at all was testimony to the fact that he had a talent and could've done well, if *he'd applied himself.* Everyone agreed, with his good looks and enormous confidence, he had the makings of a big-time salesman. He could've graduated to cars, maybe real estate. And soon it became clear that the economy was rebounding beyond all expectations, everywhere the country was building up. Up! America's arms were outstretched, eager for my uncle to introduce his charm into the Middle West. Now was the time! My father, who'd spent the war stationed in Virginia, driving a shiploader, came home and found a job right away in Seymour's new lumberyard—a growing concern—my father and his strong back had a future. But as for Uncle Rod— what could you do for a man who said he preferred to go to the ballpark, and then, brazenly, without the slightest hint of remorse, he did!

He traveled; after two years back in Illinois he decided to visit Albert Livingstone. The letter he'd received in the hospital had impressed him very much. Never had he read such an earnest, eloquent message. That Albert Livingstone was a sensitive soul there could be no doubt; he offered his deepest sympathies, and unfettered friendship; you couldn't ask for a nicer fellow to shoot you through the neck. My uncle carried the letter folded up in his wallet, and at family gatherings after the dessert plates had been pushed aside would read it aloud. The part near the end, "In our hands we hold too many truths, the triggers of unknown destinies," my grandmother always made him read twice, though she knew it by heart, and had been heard to repeat it to herself while working over the sink, cutting the bruises out of apples.

Through the VA Uncle Rod learned that Albert Livingstone lived in a small town in northwestern Pennsylvania, a place called Manfred. Uncle Rod drove for two days to get there, looked up the address in the local telephone book, and soon was standing at his door. Before knocking he wrapped a black scarf around his neck. An older woman answered—Albert's mother, it turned out, once he was inside and the introductions began. She lived with Albert. Uncle Rod had first identified himself as an old friend from the Army, but Albert, a roundfaced young man with a cleft in his chin (so big you could stick a coin in, easy as a pair of loafers, according to Uncle Rod)—Albert began to apologize, for he didn't recognize my uncle, and asked his name.

When Uncle Rod told him, Albert Livingstone's expression changed. Petrified. All of a sudden he looked like a fish, my uncle claimed—like after you catch it, and you hit it over the head with the butt of your knife, before cutting it open. That's how his eyes went, all glassy. Like a stunned fish.

"P-please sit d-down," Albert stammered.

Rod made himself comfortable while Albert's mother brought them coffee and wedges of spice cake. My uncle asked Albert how he was doing, and Albert answered faintly, "Fine . . ." Upon being pressed, Albert revealed that he was going back to college with the new government money, which didn't surprise Uncle Rod in the least. Anybody could see he was a smart fellow, even with his stunned fish eyes, which kept moving down to the scarf around my uncle's neck, then looking away . . . but always, coming back.

Sitting up very straight, Albert inquired, "What, uh, are you doing now? How is your health? Are you feeling—is your condition—all right?"

By now Albert's mother had joined them. She was a squat little woman and anybody could see that in thirty years Albert would look just like her.

My uncle didn't answer Albert's question straightaway but complimented Mrs. Livingstone on her spice cake, which was surely the finest spice cake he'd ever eaten, so moist, unlike any other spice cake you cared to talk about, which stuck in your throat, a very unpleasant experience, you could say painful, defeating all enjoyment—why would a person even offer something that stuck in your throat? But her spice cake wasn't like that, he wanted her to know; it was a true privilege to fork it into his mouth: so moist. "Isn't that right, Albert?"

Albert nodded, staring at my uncle.

"I s'pose you're wondering why I wear this scarf around my neck?" my uncle asked.

When Albert heard this, a shudder went through him, he gasped and flopped once in his chair. Albert's mother turned and told my uncle she thought it made Army men look dashing. She blushed.

"Because if I don't," Uncle Rod said, "MY HEAD FALLS OFF! HAH HAH HAH HAH!"

Albert's mother looked at him, her lips working, then to Uncle Rod's horror, Albert Livingstone began to cry. "What is this?" his mother said, in a high panicky voice. Uncle Rod stood up. *"What is this?"* she repeated, and would continue to do so for the next few minutes, over and over, so that it almost drove Uncle Rod crazy, *"What is this?"* while he was trying to communicate with Albert. My uncle rushed to him, saying he was sorry, he was really all right—he started pulling at the scarf around his neck. Albert threw his hands up in front of his face.

"No, no!"

"What is this?"

"Look, Albert, look. There's hardly nothing—I got a beautiful neck! Really, look!"

"No, no!"

Uncle Rod had to corner him on the couch: "Albert, Albert! I'm healed, I'm a new man, don't you see?" *"What is this?"* "No, no!"; till eventually Albert saw, was reassured, and then, the struggle over, wrapped his arms around his chest, panting. The flush on his face became blotches. But even as Albert calmed down, and they straightened the cushions, his mother became ever more distraught, insisting, to the point that Uncle Rod wondered aloud if he should leave. Albert nodded briskly, agreeing this would be for the best, so after a hasty squeeze of the hand and a final wave through the door, Uncle Rod got back in his car and drove away from Manfred, Pennsylvania, vowing never to forget this day. An hour down the road he stopped at a roadside diner where he took the letter out of his wallet and read it, one more time, and began to cry.

To his amazement when he returned to Illinois there was another letter from Albert Livingstone waiting for him, in which he professed his regrets. And with such courtesy! Thereafter my uncle received a Christmas card every year from Albert Livingstone, with a short account of what was happening in Albert's life, and with cordial wishes for Uncle Rod's own. "You feel important just reading his words," Uncle Rod observed. "He means them. It's more than just nicey-nice shit." No one would've dreamed of saying anything critical of Albert Livingstone in my uncle's presence, for he respected the man who'd almost killed him with a devotion bordering on reverence.

*

My uncle told the story many times of what happened that day in Manfred, not because he liked talking about himself, as some say, puffing himself up, but by way of personal explanation, and humility, for it was after that day and the tears he caused that he resolved never again to tell a joke (and everyone in the family can attest to his faithfulness to his resolution, and to how much Uncle Rod loved jokes) with a punch line.

Above all, from that day he seemed more conscious of the future, and ready to experiment with it. He wasn't just out to make merry. Truth was, his battle with Death was only beginning. He abandoned selling entirely for a time to size up his possibilities, announcing that there ought to be a worthier way to make a go of it, a more fundamental destiny, here in the heartland. Eventually he ran out of cash and his car was repossessed, so he took a job in a squeaking training gym in Chicago where he ran a towel service and carried buckets of crushed ice. One day, when three fighters in a row showed up drunk, he was asked to try his hand as a sparring partner. Thus began Uncle Rod's short (and famous, in our family) career as a boxer.

He didn't go very far, wasn't particularly good, but at the start scored some local upsets. Once the Sunday *Tribune* printed a large action photo of Uncle Rod in its Sports Spotlight, "Big Rod pummels Harlan (the Hammer) Hancock," which created a sensation in the family, thoroughly redeemed him, gave rise to wild, unfounded hopes—which just as quickly evaporated. To all this Uncle Rod shrugged. Even if he'd fought his way to the top, he reminded, there were never any fat dream purses to be won at bantamweight.

Still, Uncle Rod's boxing days are remembered by some in the family as his apex, for after his retirement from the ring his choice in professions as well as his conduct became, in their eyes, less and less respectable. He still wasn't married, preferring instead a series of female "little friends," as Grandma called them (the burgeoning sentimental side of his life—more on that to come), and at this time he established his first contacts with the Van Allen School of Mortuary Science, which later, for other reasons now too well known and controversial, proved so unfortunate. At this time he simply worked as a model. "It was easy money," he always said.

2

Introducing Me

(Learning to Cry for Someone Other Than

Myself)

My first memories of Uncle Rod are happy ones. He was very good to us children. I was still small, my brother Raymond still yowled pinkishly in his crib, dangling his head between the bars. It was after a Sunday dinner, I recall, when Raymond finally fell asleep and we went outside to sit in the backyard in the shade where the gnats were terrible. They attacked your ears, flew in your mouth. A neighbor's dog was barking hysterically, probably the snap-and-tear death of another ground squirrel, and we worried the commotion would wake Raymond. I remember that I felt like crying as I clutched a book to my ribs and tried to spit out a dead gnat.

Oh, those Sunday afternoons! It was all too clear, they were designed expressly to drain the sweet juice out of life. This particular Sunday was interminable, so hot and sticky, so boring, with the gnats and grown-ups who just kept on talking, talking, for hours and hours, despite the gnats: it was inconceivable how they could find so much to say.

Yes, I wanted to cry. Today there was something in the tone of their voices that touched me deep inside, made my throat constrict, even though I didn't follow their meaning. Inflections of anger, mistrust, which I instinctively recoiled from and wished they would stop.

Yes, please stop! Why did they carry on so? Years later my father told me their conversation had to do with a lie Uncle Rod had told, about money; my father had lent him $200 to pay for a divorce, for a marriage that had lasted six weeks, but Uncle Rod had invested the money instead in his new business, color TV converters.

Few people remember color TV converters anymore. This was when color TV was still a novelty, and most people couldn't afford one. Rod was selling a kit to help others convert their old black-and-white sets to color. The kit included a frame, adjustable to fit any size of TV, and a pliable rectangle of tinted, transparent celluloid. The celluloid was multicolored: the top was blue, which gradually became lighter toward the middle, where there was a band of pale yellowish grey, which further down took on a greenish hue, till the bottom became solid green. You fixed the converter over the screen of your black-and-white TV, and you had color. It worked best for programs like westerns, where there were plenty of outdoor scenes. Uncle Rod was big on the idea and might've made a lot of money if he'd had more support, but my father scoffed and wouldn't help him anymore. Even in later years my uncle defended the gadget, saying it had become a collector's item.

But at this time in the humid yard I understood none of my elders' reasonings but simply felt their tone, the grief it carried, in the same way I judged certain kinds of music to be sad. The tone transformed my surroundings so that suddenly our house looked sad, the ferns and broad dusty leaves of rhubarb by the back steps, the drainpipe that tilted crazily off its brace. Squinting against the light, scratching at my mosquito bites, I raked my fingernails methodically over weeping bumps till my brain slipped into a fog of pleasure—*oh, oh, I loved it*—this drove the sadness away. But not for long. When the pleasure wore off, the bites' after-sting made me gasp; my, the scalding!

In desperation, gripping my book between my knees while I blew on my arm, I began to cry. Not from the welts as much as from the fact that they were *still* talking, their voices continued to oppress me, that tone would not stop. Even after pleasure the tug of sadness persisted. A little bird hopped on the grass in front of me, and an image came to mind of this bird without legs, on its belly. Unable to hop—someone had cut off its legs. I began to cry harder. Deathbelly. I wasn't a mean person, I liked this bird. Who in my head had cut off its legs? Uncle Rod and my father broke off their conversation, and looked at me. "What is it, Judy?" my father asked. "Judy?" But he didn't get out of his lawn chair. I turned my back on them, and the bird flew away.

When someone touched my shoulder, to my surprise it was my uncle. "What ya got there?" he asked, pulling at my book.

I moved away, not letting him have it.

"Judy?"

He received no answer. I was busy crying, and besides, nobody was allowed to touch my dinosaur book. Though I was just beginning to read and the text was too hard for me, I adored the pictures, the huge green beasts and enormous wavy plants and shimmering aquarium skies: I liked too the stark black-and-white photographic plates in the back, showing reconstructed bones, proving (as I'd made my parents repeat many times) these monsters were not make-believe. They were *true*. This idea was wonderful, awe-inspiring; real monsters were a source of great comfort to me. I carried my dinosaur book with me everywhere. My great-Aunt Myriam on my mother's side had tried to take it away, saying she knew something better for me—"Surely you'd prefer a dolly"—but I yanked my book free. As if it were any of her business! Dolls I already had, in fact a whole tribe of fat-limbed babies inherited from cousins in North Platte, which now covered my bedspread or were squashed between the bed and the wall. (These were being punished.) In contrast, there was only one dinosaur book.

"Keep your hands off!" I'd told her.

This surprised my great-aunt (why everyone referred to her this way was a mystery to me; frankly, I was not impressed) but it was a fact, people had no right to be touching my treasure, soiling it with their curiosity. Not only did I pull away from my uncle—I ran around to the other side of a lilac bush.

But he followed me, ducking the clothesline, repeating his question. "Judy?" He knelt in front of me and looked me in the eye. He didn't try to grab. "Please. Won't you show me?" He asked very politely, the gentleness in his voice like a sweet breeze on my face. What could I do?

He smiled, waiting.

In the end I let him take a peek, and explained to him about the bones in the back. Uncle Rod seemed very interested. I watched his face, and even then, in the same way that I understood the tones of adult voices, his fine jaw and ears communicated something to me, an idea that had eluded me until now, which was suddenly manifest under my eyes, affecting me strongly: the idea of *handsome*. I forgot to be afraid.

"You ever find a dinosaur bone?" he asked.

I shook my head.

"You haven't? You ever look for a dinosaur bone?"

"No," I said softly, shy under his gaze. Actually, it had never occurred to me to look for a dinosaur bone.

"Really? You never looked for a dinosaur bone! Well, I'd say it's high time."

And he walked off. Past me, past my father who was unsticking his shirt from the back of his lawn chair, over to the toolshed. He emerged with a spade and a hoe, and came back to me, a spring in his step. "Let's go, honey," he said. I didn't move, unbelieving. A gnat buzzed in

22

my ear and I slapped myself. He shrugged and headed off to a sunny spot in the middle of the backyard. He threw the hoe in the grass, and lifted the spade in the air, eyeing the ground. Then he brought it down with an *umph*. He lifted again, *umph*. *Umph*. Then he levered the spade, and a neat circle of sod and earth popped up, rolled aside like a lid. With short violent jabs he drove the spade around the hole, making it bigger, then scooped out the loose dirt. Sweat began to bead on his face.

"Whadya think you're doing?" my father called.

He didn't look up, but replied, "I'm gonna dig this girl a dinosaur."

Suddenly I was running to his side in the sun, where I seized the hoe and began to scratch at the ground.

"Come on," my father said, "don't tease her."

Uncle Rod grunted.

"I ain't teasing her."

"We'll find a dinosaur?" I asked, scraping frantically, exposing grass roots.

He heaved aside a huge scoop, then plunged the spade again, working it deeper with his sturdy muscles. "Maybe," he said, "maybe." Then to my father: "Why don't you join us, Carlton?"

My father twisted out of his chair and stepped into the sun, answering, "Just knock it off. You hear me? That's my grass there, fella. You think you're funny? Well you don't know funny."

That *tone* in his voice—the same as their argument minutes before, as if my father insisted on spoiling things. I couldn't bear it, and wished he'd be quiet. Either he should help us or leave us alone.

My mother came out. "What are they doing?"

"They're tearing the hell out of the yard," my father said, hands on his hips, "what does it look like?"

"We're digging up a dinosaur!" I said.

"Oh," my mother said.

"Listen," my father told me, in a softer voice, "he's only kidding you, understand? You won't really find a dinosaur, not here. He's doing this for . . . for *me*. And it's a silly idea! So please, Judy, stop hurting the grass."

I paused, turned to Uncle Rod. He was standing in the hole, now almost up to his knees. Widening it around him, chopping at the earth. He huffed; his shirt-tail popped out. My uncle didn't look like he was kidding. He seemed to pay no attention to my father. Sweat streamed down his face.

My mother came around in front, standing toe to toe with my uncle, but at a level above. She remarked, "I've never seen you work so hard, Rod."

For an instant there was a hitch in his movement—then he swung up another spray of dirt. Still digging, he answered with averted eyes. "Well, Annie, it's like this. I owe my brother here some money; two hundred dollars, to be exact. I imagine you already know about that? Maybe you talked about it? So I guess you could say I'm offering my services."

"Services? You've made your point. Enough is enough!" my father said. His face was red and sweating, too, though he wasn't doing a thing.

"Only he doesn't always appreciate my services," Uncle Rod went on. "That puts me in a bind. Lucky for me there's Judy here. Big Rod is glad to help her out. Isn't that right?" He smiled at me. "Dig, honey."

I started in again with the hoe. My mother said to no one in particular that she wondered about me, how much Rod was paying me, or if it was *free*? Were my services bargained for? Or were they just *taken*? Then she added she'd better go check up on Raymond, and headed back to the house. My father stormed after her.

"Annie!"

As far as I was concerned it was perfectly simple: my uncle was doing me a favor—of course he shouldn't pay me! We worked until Uncle Rod was in almost

24

waist-deep, while I'd made a crooked furrow beside him, halfway around the circle. Then we stopped, panting. He threw the spade on the pile of dirt and coughed a little, his chest going up and down. He spat. He opened and closed his hands; with his fists he punched at the air, a flurry, then stopped, laughing. He reached into his shirt pocket and pulled out a pack of cigarettes, stuck one in the corner of his mouth. I laughed too, though I didn't know why. My palms hurt.

"Have you ever seen a live dinosaur?" I asked.

Now, I knew there were no live dinosaurs—no such thing—but I was testing my uncle. To be sure.

"No," he said, to my relief. He went on to explain that they were extinct, had been for many, many years, which my parents had already told me so it was old stuff and probably in the book, too, but I listened without interrupting. I didn't mind hearing it again. Then:

"Why are they extinct?" I asked.

He hesitated. The back screen door slammed, my father walked toward us, glowering. "It just happens that way, Judy. Everything becomes extinct, somewhere down the line."

I shook my head.

"But not people," I said. "People won't become extinct. Not people!"

"What in God's name are you telling this child?" my father exclaimed. "I don't want you filling her head with nonsense. This has gone as far as it can go."

"Will they?" I asked, looking back and forth between them, "will people become extinct?"

"No, no, no," my father said.

Uncle Rod chuckled. "You read the papers, Carlton?" And he reached for his shovel and resumed digging.

"OUT of here!" my father roared, pointing. "OUT of my yard!"

My tears came, not because of Uncle Rod as my

25

father supposed, but because of this tone, again, a tone so harsh, and the fact that I didn't know what to believe, or whom, there were no answers that inspired trust. Why were grown-ups this way, why did they behave so badly? The sight of my tears infuriated my father even more, and he began to cuss my uncle and kick dirt back in the hole around him. "Goddamnit, Goddamnit!" he cried. The dirt flew; Uncle Rod dropped his spade, put his hands before him, covering himself, at one point flinching, "Ow!" He reached down in the hole. "Stop it, Carlton." He held up a dirty yellow object. "A bone!" he shouted. "A bone!" For an instant my father hesitated, then with a terrible oath started kicking the dirt with renewed fury. Uncle Rod climbed out of the hole and brought it over to me.

"Look, look, a dinosaur bone!"

"It's a dog bone! I mean a steak bone," my father said, gasping. He stumbled toward us.

"No, no, it's a dinosaur bone," Uncle Rod insisted, pressing it into my hand. I stopped crying, feeling the roughness. What was it?

"How do you know?" I asked, hiccupping.

My father's big hand came around the back of my uncle's neck. "Carlton, look close now," Uncle Rod said. "You gonna tell her that's not a dinosaur bone? Look close now."

I stared into my father's eyes. He took a deep breath, and his voice came out dry, tight: "Yes. That is a dinosaur bone."

"Looks like a kneecap to me," said Uncle Rod. "Wipe it there, isn't a beauty? It might be extinct but it's a beauty, you gotta admit, it's a beauty, isn't it?"

"Yes—yes," I breathed, gripping the bone, looking back and forth in admiration from it to my uncle with the unlit, bent cigarette in the corner of his mouth, a dirt-streaked, handsome face.

3

Purple Heart in Exile

No, he was not lazy. Perhaps he was not steady like my father at the lumberyard but he pursued his ideas with great energy, at least toward the end of a project when he had to bail it out. He knew how to duck and scramble, let the punches whistle past him, and actually seemed to enjoy himself most when doing so. My grandfather attributed Uncle Rod's lifestyle to a lack of intelligence, but this was partly a misunderstanding: Uncle Rod had raised Grandpa's ire by declaring that as far as he was concerned, he was descended from a race of idiots.

Now, my grandfather was extremely proud of his Scottish ancestry, his purity, and liked to gloat about it. "Pure, pure 100% Scottish!" he cried for everyone to hear, squeezing his arms and knees, "that's right, the real thing, undiluted, not even a drop of English in me!" He slapped his cheeks, chucked himself under the chin, pinched his shoulders, smiling with his small, worn-down teeth. He couldn't stop touching himself, and was quick to blame any doubtful qualities in his sons on my grandmother, speaking frankly of her as "part Polack, part Eye-talian, part hillbilly, and if the truth be known even a few dribs of nigger." This last my grandmother always objected to, gathering herself up with indignation. Flushed, looking as if she might cry, she insisted it was Cherokee, a trace of Cherokee blood she had, just a titch—but Grandpa would not be moved, conceding that though maybe, for all we knew, there might be some Cherokee, it didn't blot out the nigger. "What about your great-grandad Alphonse?" he would bark, and that did it, Grandma clutched her stomach in front of her. Her chin started to tremble. Then the silent weeping. Grandpa cackled, hee-hee-hee, pinching himself. He was keen on genealogy.

As far as I could tell, I didn't resemble that side of the family anyway. I looked more like my mother, who was Irish. Grandpa hinted at Jewishness in her people, too, but she didn't know about that. She liked to repeat the story from the old country of her great-grandmother Olivine who, after picking out her tombstone, found herself so poor that she couldn't afford to have her entire name engraved on it, and had to settle for O. This attracted her notice in her final resting place such as she'd never enjoyed in her lifetime, and in the generations that followed she was pointed out to visitors of the village, and no doubt still was, to this very day. Probably the most famous of my ancestors. (How many times I heard my mother recount this story, I can't begin to calculate.) Grandpa, jealous of others' anecdotes, came back to the subject of Jewishness. "Listen, I can *see* it," he announced, "that don't get past me." Once, after hearing Grandpa go on about being a Scot, I asked Uncle Rod what I was.

"You?" he said, laughing. "You're just a bastard American."

"Watch your tongue!" my mother exclaimed.

I was confused. My grandfather nodded at me, soberly. Grandma gathered herself up, but didn't say a thing. Uncle Rod wanted to know if genes had anything to do with his painful sinuses, for which he'd found neither cure nor relief except when he was a boxer, and got hit repeatedly in the face. It was then that he let slip the remark, that in any case, as far as he was concerned he was descended from a race of idiots.

28

The effect of these words was like a giant flashbulb exploding. We froze, and for an instant time itself was illuminated, centuries of accumulated Gasses. My! Then the moment faded and we found ourselves blinking at my uncle.

My grandfather raised his fist, shook his head, and declared that some people didn't appreciate quality, or the fineness of life, some people didn't know shit from apple butter—then, in case no one had heard before, announced that he was One hundred per cent Scottish, One hundred per cent. Hitting his fist on his knee. Though now Uncle Rod insisted, "I'm talking about the human race, I mean the human race."

After the color TV converters went bust, he was unemployed for a few months before taking a job at a dog kennel. Here he devoted himself to his charges, lengthening their run and improving the menu, but before long wearied of so much yapping, so many, many turds, so he quit and moved on to a job as a mail sorter, which he got by reading in the local paper about a man who had died of food poisoning and going to apply for his position immediately after. He lasted over a year, which raised hopes he would get hired proper by the Post Office, an honorable profession with security, benefits, a slew of paid holidays—all a person could ask for! Grandma said she could picture him in a blue uniform. But then Uncle Rod hit upon the idea of chocolate Jesus.

It seemed a natural. The Christmas season was approaching, heralded as always by a gilded card from Albert Livingstone on the heels of Thanksgiving, wishing my uncle prosperity. This year Albert's card triggered memories that took on new significance. In fact Rod's mind was suddenly afire with inspiration. He'd seen chocolate Jesuses in France back in his Army days when he was in the hospital, though at the time, with all the shortages, they weren't made out of real chocolate. Even the lower grade almond-patty variety were in scarce supply. He lay in the sun-washed ward of Tauzé Le Mignon and listened to natives speak wistfully of the wonderful chocolate Jesuses before the war; it was a pity the children would be denied them yet another Christmas. He tried one of the imitation dark doughy Jesuses circulating at the time, and though they were objects of derision among the French, who insisted on either a real chocolate Jesus or none at all, Uncle Rod liked it; not a bad little treat, not bad in the least. One day as he lay in bed and loosened the bandage around his wound he polished off four in a row; Frenchmen in his ward gladly traded theirs for cigarettes. Uncle Rod credited chocolate Jesus, even in the imitation form, with his speedy recovery.

So when, over twenty years later while sorting a mountain of holiday mail, the idea struck him to put chocolate Jesus on the market in America—why, it seemed a godsend! The product had already proven its appeal; and here was a big market, a tremendous market, people spending money for the holidays as if they were out of their minds! Chocolate Jesus was just begging to be introduced.

He quit his job. He drew up plans. He found a baker on Melbourne Avenue off Lake Michigan who also dabbled in chocolate molds, and within three days was peddling chocolate Jesus to grocers, tea rooms, and delicatessens all over Chicago, in the suburbs and back in our hometown. Of course, many shops refused him; there are plenty of people who balk at a new idea. But enough interest was generated and enough shops took him on that within a week he was operating at a profit. He hustled all day and into the night making it work; no one could say he was a loafer, or lacked drive: here was proof to the contrary. And though he didn't pay back my father the money he owed him, he bought our family an enormous new black-and-white TV set, complete with converter, which certainly put him back more than $200.

My father looked up the model in catalogs, and checked at dealers, and concluded that his brother had spent almost twice his debt. No, Rod wasn't stingy, my father said, you couldn't accuse him of that.

The chocolate Jesuses came in three sizes, all of them sold in a cardboard cradle ("It's a manger," Uncle Rod insisted, "a manger," though everyone agreed it looked like a cradle; still, we found it darling). At our house we had a free supply of the chocolate Jesuses, and it was like a dream for Raymond and me, eating gluey babies in the morning, in the afternoon, evenings.

"Gotta give Rod credit," my father said, dipping one in his coffee, "the little guy's scored this time."

My mother said they were fattening, but sneaked the mini size when she thought no one was looking. Grandma and Grandpa took a box back to their house, because if you sucked, you didn't have to chew them.

We wondered what my uncle would do with all his money. My father speculated that he would buy a new car, the kind with the radio antenna that went up and down when you pushed a button on the dash—that was just like Rod. My mother said if he had any sense he would make a down payment on a house—was it conceivable, even, that he might buy one outright? Maybe I wasn't very smart but I remember telling Raymond that Uncle Rod just might become President. Raymond bit into another, giggling, his teeth brown and dripping. Anything seemed possible.

Jingle bells,

I taught my brother to sing as I'd learned in school,

Shotgun shells,
Grandma laid
An egg.

A giddy, giddy time!

31

"Look at that, would you look at that!" my father exclaimed, hitting his head with the heel of his hand. He was watching his new TV. On a peaceful village blue snow fell, the roofs of the houses were covered with yellow, the streets drifting green. My mother nodded in her chair:

"It surely is something."

"I had a dream like that once!" I put in.

"Here comes the bear!" my father said. "Would you look at that? Tutti frutti! Oh Lord!"

My uncle came back from the kitchen, bringing a piece of custard pie on a plate. He sat down, smiling, and as I watched him attack his dessert, oh, how I loved him!

"I'm glad to see you're getting in the spirit of things," he told us.

"This kills me," my father gasped.

"Judy, tell your brother to come here and see this," my mother said. "These Christmas specials are wonderful."

That evening, none of us felt any shame. We were listening only to our hearts, and liked what we found there. When did everything begin to fall apart?

In the beginning we were caught by surprise. The Rev. Marty Stewart of the First Church of Christ Resurrected was the first to publicly protest. His letter to a suburban daily attracted the attention of other clergy to the spread of chocolate Jesus in the Metro area. It was blasphemy, Rev. Stewart said, a craven, obscene affront to the most cherished manifestation of divine gentleness and the well-spring of all goodwill and peace on earth. Would people stand for it?

We soon found out. Forces were joined. The Presbyterians, Espicopalians, and Methodists came out against it; the Baptists and Assembly of God congregations organized a boycott of all stores that sold the daemonic totem. The Sisters of Upper Winsiccola issued a press release. Two aldermen expressed their horror, though mercifully the mayor of Chicago, whom my fathered admired greatly, was out of town.

Uncle Rod's picture was in the newspaper again. This time, however, none of the excitement gripped the family as for his boxing exploits years before. A hush gathered in our house, for it was impossible not to feel the force of accumulated ill will. Though the Christmas cards kept coming and there was a blanket of fresh snow onto which Christmas lights bled enthusiastically, nasty spirits were in the air, and once you breathed them, they began to work on you. You started wondering if maybe you really were low-down. The Sunday before Christmas we felt terribly nervous that we would hear our name denounced from the pulpit of our own church.

My father let it be known that he'd rather stay home. "But we'll look guilty if we don't go," my mother said. "We *have* to go."

What a relief it was to be spared, though after the sermon that Sunday my father remarked that if Fat Boy had dared breathe a word (he sometimes referred to our pastor in this way, but it wasn't unkind), or utter even a syllable after everything my mother had done for the church, he and Fat Boy would've had it out, man to man.

All the same Grandma, who made it only to the following February before she died, said she couldn't help it, she was ashamed. She died ashamed. Grandpa, though never a particularly religious man, said Rod had no right to upset innocent people like that. There were a lot of creeds out there, and a fella ought to respect them all. What angered my parents most was Uncle Rod's attitude in the newspapers: he was smug, vaunting his idea, which no one had brought to this country before. He allowed himself to be photographed with a wide grin, holding up one of the beleaguered Jesuses. He acted as if the whole affair would blow over, maybe even help as good advertising. He had no real grasp of the resistance

33

mounting not only to his Jesus, but to him personally. Slogans intended to be catchy, like "Why can't transubstantiation be tasty?", left him a target, his detractors, the press, the formerly indifferent—everyone—without a drop of mercy.

The stores dropped Jesus like a plague. At the same time Uncle Rod's phone began to ring. There were threats. Did he think such disrespect would go unpunished? Did he think he would get away with this? *He would see! He would see!* One repeat caller, who identified himself only as The Angel, warned him constantly how many days there were until Christmas.

At our house the atmosphere worsened too. Our phone also began to ring, and we had to pretend that our last name was just a coincidence. Who? Who? Oh no, not us! My parents took me to school in the car; Raymond wasn't allowed to play in the yard, though he longed to make a snowman, and pressed his cheek to the windowpane, crying for our attention.

"Oh for heaven's sake . . . let him make his GODDAMN snowman!" my father exploded on the sparkling afternoon before the big day.

"No—you see that blue car that just went past?" my mother said, peering through the blinds. "That's the second time. I think they're watching us."

"I'm not sure I believe that, Annie."

"Are you going to take that risk? Are you?"

"Listen, I'll get Dad's old twenty gauge from downstairs, and go stand beside him while he rolls it. Then will you feel better?"

"Don't be ridiculous. You'll do no such thing."

My father went outside without a jacket and in the biting air packed together a big snowball, as large as Raymond's head, then brought it into the house, shivering and trying to knock the white off his shoes and socks. "HERE!" he barked at Raymond, who eyed the snowball and didn't really want to take it, I could see,

34

but was wise enough to reach for it before my father said something else. He clutched the snowball with both hands, apprehension swirling on his face while my father dug snow from inside his shoe with his finger, muttering. I observed him and thought how my uncle would never put himself in such a situation—he wore tall brown leather boots, very fine, of which he was proud and took great care, shining them several times a week. He'd told me how he'd had wet feet for months at a stretch in the Army, and now he intended never to put his sinuses through that again. I'd bought him a kit with a jar of boot polish as a Christmas present . . . .

Raymond bit the snowball.

"Oh Lord. Watch out for twigs," my father said.

When my parents went to their room to continue their argument in private, I was supposed to keep an eye on my brother. (My mother, speaking low and looking warily as she put the poinsettia on a shelf: "It's poisonous, you know.") Left alone with me, Raymond began to complain that his hands were cold, that he didn't know what to do with it, his wrists were numbing, too, and his forearms, and soon I couldn't stand it any longer, his whining, the fact that he was so weak: hey, I didn't want to hold his stupid snowball! Was it my fault if he'd wanted one? Then to distract him I made up a story about a family of reindeer that might be seen trotting up and down our back alley, if only we could go outside to watch. Oh, dear, wasn't it a pity we couldn't? Upon hearing this, Raymond's face began to churn. Raising his hands above his head, suddenly he dashed the snowball to the floor. His breast stained, he thrust his dripping fingers into his mouth and with a squeaking sound started stomping circles around the carpet. At this point I left him and went upstairs to my room, closed the door and played *Saint Wenceslaus' Choir Sings Your Favorite Christmas Carols* on my box record player at high volume, so high that it was impossible to think.

By then, maybe only Uncle Rod could've set things

right at our house. Surely we had gone awfully wrong. But the Chief of Police had called on my uncle, advised him to clear out of town and go spend Christmas Eve alone in a strange place where nobody knew him. In the interest of public safety. Uncle Rod had heeded his warning.

So the night before Christmas turned out to be the grimmest of all. At the time I couldn't comprehend everything that was happening, though I'd grasped that the situation was very grave, and certainly my uncle would never be President; the phone calls, especially the threats, I understood only later. All I knew for sure was that Grandma was in grief, stuffing tissues up her sleeve, sitting on the edge of the couch in a pained, hunched-over position, and that Uncle Rod had been compelled to go away and avoid Christmas Eve with us. He telephoned from a motor lodge in Urbana. He'd found a room with a tree.

I *had* read the controversial newspaper article about him, for I'd found it a few days before in Mom and Dad's top dresser drawer when I was snooping around for unwrapped Christmas presents. Why hide this? I'd wondered, recognizing at once the grinning man in the photograph. In my parents' room on the sly, reading the clipping in great haste, I missed its real meaning. The article talked about chocolate Jesus, Uncle Rod, France. In one paragraph Uncle Rod said he had a Purple Heart.

That was the part that stuck with me. In the final countdown as the hours ticked closer and closer to full-blown and irreversible Christmas, I was haunted. A Purple Heart. How the phrase echoed in my mind, worrying. If my uncle's heart was purple—what could it mean? A purple heart! How . . . sinister. He'd had to go away—had he gone away to die? Was my uncle leaving us forever? In the picture he looked so happy with his chocolate Jesus, so pleased, and the contrast made the present situation all the more unbearable. Perhaps I'd never see him again. His face. I wouldn't get to give him his boot polish. "Rod," I whispered, "dear Rod." Oh, why did people have to go away and die? People you loved, and with Christmas there was no mercy! That night, as if to rub it in, I found a bundle of chocolate Jesuses in the wastecan.

They were tied together with an elastic band, in with the wrapping paper tubes and orange peels. *Who* had thrown them away? I asked myself. In my uncle's most dire moment, *who* could do that? My heart froze in horror at such a betrayal. My mother stood over the table, setting out plates, humming: *"Gloria! In excelsis Deo . . . "* I was shaking, staring into the wastecan, unable even to touch the chocolate Jesuses, and rescue them. For the second time in my life my tears began to roll for Uncle Rod. My mother came up behind me, rested her hand on my shoulder. "I know, dear," she said. "I know."

4

Oxygen Problems

(Not to Mention Heaven)

Uncle Rod took Grandma's funeral arrangements upon himself, organized everything, including the meal afterward. The event made a big impression on me for it was the first time I'd seen a dead person. Of course it was sad, of course I sobbed a little—but mainly I watched, with shock and fascination, the spectacle of it all. They'd taken away Grandma's glasses, and put red makeup on her cheeks such as she'd never worn before. You might've thought she was going to a party. Her mouth was very straight, lifted at the corners, the skin on her face tighter. Horrible to look yet I couldn't stop staring.

Her soul was in heaven, they said. But it seemed so weird to leave her body behind. Here, before my eyes, was a person or what looked like a person—but *a person without a soul!* Amazing.

The morning after she died in the hospital, I came downstairs into the kitchen and saw my father at the table, his head in his hands. Never, never had I seen him this way. After a few seconds he looked up, asked in a voice like a whisper, "What do you want?" He wasn't crying, though his eyes were puffy. His hair was mussed. He looked as if he'd been sleeping, there at the kitchen table. Right then it struck me that Grandma wasn't Grandma to my father, she was his mother. Of course I'd known that before, in an uncurious way, but I'd never *felt* this fact, what it meant. He even called her

Grandma: that was her name. But now, my father had no mother.

"N—nothing!" I told him, and ran out of the kitchen, looking for my own mother.

I found her in my parents' bedroom. With bobby pins between her lips she frowned at me in the mirror, for I hadn't knocked. She was already getting dressed. "Honey, you'll have to make your brother breakfast. I'm going down to the funeral home with your father. Has your uncle called?"

I shook my head. "I don't know."

"We're almost out of milk, but you can manage." She threw off her robe and moved quickly, keeping her back to me, fishing fresh underwear out of drawers. This was still in the time of pointy brassieres, with fake pearly snaps to attach, and that particular day, though it wasn't Sunday, she put on a girdle, too. "You can make cinnamon toast if you want," she said over her shoulder. When she turned around she drummed on her tummy several times with her knuckles, but it didn't go down any more. It was weird to think that I might someday have a body like this, so moundy, front and back and in between. Now she stepped into a half slip, then thrust her arms into a blouse that buttoned in back, her arms twisting spidery behind her as she said, "You'll be just fine, honey." Her eyes had dark circles. I handed her her skirt, which she slipped into while scarcely breaking a stride on her way to her dark blue shoes, which she put on with two quick jiggles of her wrist. "Be good now." She moved past me, giving her skirt a final zip up the side.

I grabbed her, put my arms around her waist. Not crying, but breathing hard.

"Judy, what is it?"

Strange how suddenly I couldn't catch my breath. My mother put her arms around me.

"I'm sorry about Grandma too. I really am."

Grandma. I was thinking about her. I wanted her to stay, stay with me that morning, and my father downstairs, too. Not leave our house. Already they were slipping away from me, already!

"Grandma had a good life . . ." she was saying. But such words were beside the point; fact was, Grandma had got away.

"Judy, I have to go." She pulled toward the door, stepping backwards. "They're waiting for us."

A few mornings later, we rode to church with my grandfather. He wore all black that day, and on the way I noticed how quiet everyone was, and how the inside of his car was cleaner than our house. The last time I'd ridden with him was in the summer with my grandmother still alive and he'd refused to let us roll down the windows and circulate some air because it was bad for gas mileage. Now I thought: "She's dead, she's dead, she's dead," with the rhythm of the wheels.

At the church, my parents made me sit next to him, for they had it in their heads that "Grandpa should be alongside youth." They could've given him Raymond, as far as I was concerned, but Raymond, The Little Prince, hadn't come with us. That morning he'd been sent to the neighbors', and while we were burying Grandma he was drinking Mrs. Gertz's cocoa and watching cartoons.

I was very fond of my grandfather but sitting next to him at Grandma's funeral was holy torture. I tried not to look at his face, the mottled cheeks and glistening blue eyes, the chicken skin around his throat, so I found myself staring down at his hands, their cracked yellow fingernails. They appeared out of place here. More than once when we'd visited him, he'd gone out to his garden and with these chalky nails broken me off a flower. (He'd never offered one to my mother, she reminded my father each time he did this, never.) *A pretty girl of mine should have a flower*, he would say, holding out a tulip or a crocus, which I would sniff even if it gave no scent, walking around the house rubbing the petals gently under my chin, for I liked the whispery feeling on my neck: sometimes an involuntary shiver ran through me. This made him laugh. "You do enjoy yourself, doncha?" In his younger days my grandfather had worked at a grain elevator as a railman, the only pure Scot on the job, he told me. Many a time he'd ridden in a caboose, which I thought sounded very agreeable, and worldly.

Now he turned to me, his voice cracking: "She was as fine a woman as ever walked God's earth."

I nodded at once (but thinking, Well, she won't be walking now) and pondered this mystery that the others seemed to ignore: this mystery of Grandma being in the box, yet not being in the box. Like a Brain Teaser in the Sunday paper.

Although Uncle Rod took care of all the funeral arrangements, the flowers and the meal afterwards in the church basement (his sleeves rolled up, sawing and slicing roast pork with a huge toothy knife as the plates came back for seconds, for thirds—usually on such occasions there were only sandwiches and coffee), the family was still miffed at him. My mother, father, Aunt Pat and her twins could talk only of how Uncle Rod had worn leather pants to church that day, and they would never forgive him.

Aunt Pat was the most affected. She kept coming back on the subject in her loud righteous voice, for it seemed to have made an impression on her. And my mother answered in her trumpet voice—after five minutes it gave you a headache to hear them. At least my mother had an excuse for talking loud, for she was partly deaf, had been since childhood and a case of scarlet fever; but Aunt Pat, she was just a bigmouth. "I hate to say it but I have to: he's not right!" She wasn't really my aunt anyway, but a more distant relation, a cousin of my mother's little brother's sister-in-law or something; she lived in our town and stopped by regularly, poking her nose. Her twins, Becky and Laura, hung on to every word their mother said, nodding. They were older than I, pretty, always dressed up, and they made me sick. Right then and there I decided there must be something interesting about leather pants, if Aunt Pat and the twins were so strongly set against them. They were curious about his life, too, and how he supported himself.

"You name it, he's tried all kinds of ways," my mother told them, "I've never known anyone like him. He depends a lot on other people."

Aunt Pat kept piling on question after question while Becky and Laura tried to calm their agitated little dog under the chairs—Brucie, a shivery, well-manicured Pomeranian who traveled everywhere with them and later, at a Fourth of July picnic, died a violent death. I remember morosely squeezing my fingers, watching Brucie bounce up and down, wishing for a way to get rid of these people. Why did they insist on coming round here? My mother, who was always vague about Aunt Pat's husband, a piano tuner we never saw (like many piano tuners, I later learned, he drank), spoke favorably of Aunt Pat and her daughters' appearance, how ladylike they were, always wearing dresses, you never saw them in anything else, though I wanted to tell them, "You would all look better in muzzles!"

What if I said that now? Picturing them thus equipped, the desire seized me. Oh, to tell them those words. To their busy faces! Yes! Then, would Aunt Pat blat?

Lost in this reverie, and enjoying especially the image of buckling the straps myself, I began to giggle under my hands.

My mother and Aunt Pat stopped talking. With the twins, they looked at me. Yes?

I froze. This was my chance . . . . But their eyes put

me off balance, made me anything but brash, and I tried to cover my confusion by pretending to be amused by Brucie. I bent toward him.

"Wahf! Wahf!" I said.

This startled them. Now they looked askance, their wrists moving on their laps. They thought I was peculiar.

From that day, they always would.

In fact, the aftermath of Grandma's funeral was so great that soon Uncle Rod left us entirely. I remember him drinking coffee with my father, getting up suddenly and going to the sink. There was a hardened expression on his face, his cup slid in with a clatter, and he turned away. When he left, my father came to my mother and said, "Well, Annie, it's Florida."

After the first few months, I can't say that I missed him. Florida was too far away to bother my head about, a place of postcard beaches, brilliant sands—it hardly seemed real. My uncle was off in the same hazy distance as my grandmother up in heaven, whom I pictured surrounded by white light and fat naked babes. Turning. Rod in Florida—it was the same.

Here in Seymour I had other distractions. Here, under our own roof, Raymond had become my tormentor. There were times, I must confess, when I would've been happy to choke my little brother, choke him till his eyes bulged, till his tongue hung out and his brain, which I pictured as resembling raw hamburger, would have less oxygen. Then, for once, Raymond would see more clearly, and behave as if he had a little sense. I was convinced that his brain suffered from too much oxygen, oxygen being a subject I knew about, for I studied it in school. An oxygen surplus was what made him so excitable, so emotional, so impossible. How I longed to conduct a few experiments with my hands around his neck.

But of course, my parents wouldn't let me, getting a

grip on Baby Boy was out of the question. Instead, I was supposed to watch after Raymond, protect him, keep him contented. Be his slave. Above all, keep him from crying and making a nuisance of himself. This last was something my mother and my father were incapable of doing, yet they demanded it of me. (Wasn't *me* in the department store with Raymond the time he panicked, accidently shit in the display toilet in housewares—no, it was my parents; the salesman was mortified.)

If Raymond wasn't happy, which was most of the time, the only way he knew how to express himself was to cry. He cried so easily! Not just when he fell down or bumped his big round head, but for the smallest things, when wind got in his ear, or when his favorite TV show ended. (He hogged the TV, just hogged it.) Once, and this is no lie, I looked at him across the room—and he burst out bawling.

"What did you do?" my mother asked. "What did you do?"

"Nothing! I just looked at him."

"Oh come now. You don't expect me to believe that. *Do* something for him."

And she left the room. Raymond still bawling, looking at me, enjoying himself. A little sicko, a chronic nosepicker in astronaut pajamas!

My mother told me how she loved her brother. She sat me down on the couch for a little talk, put her hand on my knee and spoke of her childhood. When she was my age, she said, she used to clean her brother's shoes. She liked it. It was a sister's responsibility, an important part of growing up. In fact, one of the brightest moments of her youth. She shivered with nostalgia at the very thought: cleaning her brother's shoes. And now he lived in North Platte, Nebraska, a prosperous roofer in a place of many tornadoes, and she never saw him. She missed him so.

"Why doesn't he send you his shoes in the mail?" I

asked, but moved away quickly. She had that look in her eye. Ready to slap.

"Listen, Miss Lip, that might happen to you someday," she said, "you might not always have your brother."

So at least there was hope. As far as I was concerned, Raymond could *lick* my shoes. Might do his oxygen problem some good. And next I would break my glass frog full of pennies and some silver to send him to North Platte, Nebraska, or if I had enough money even Juneau, Alaska, which I'd spotted on the U.S. map on the back of my school binder, a red dot, tickling my fancy. I liked Juneau. Yes, Raymond in Juneau. I had the strongest presentiment that he belonged there.

"You got your wool socks ready?" I might ask him.

"What do you mean? Why do you always say that? What do you mean?"

"And a heavy hat?"

"What do you mean? Tell me!"

I smiled mysteriously.

Still, other times I felt guilty, wondered if my mother had a point. Maybe there *was* something wrong with me. She was always helping others, thinking of their needs. She was good at being good, in fact she made it look easy. While for me it was such an effort! I might look like her—but inside, was I different? When my turn came, would I join her and Grandma and all those other weirdly good people up in heaven?

If I couldn't play with Raymond, I reasoned, maybe I should try to help him. This would not only be beneficial for Raymond but my mother would approve, too. Despite our arguments, sometimes I positively ached to please her.

"Come here, this is for you," I told my brother one day when he sat on the couch with a wet finger in his mouth, jiggling back and forth. He looked with curiosity at the string I held out.

"What's that for?"

"Your tooth. We'll tie one end around your tooth, the other end to a doorknob. Then we'll slam the door."

Already I felt more responsible, sure of myself. This was something we could do together.

He shifted his position nervously. "Gee—I don't know."

"Wouldn't you like to get it over with quick? It'll be less painful than what you're doing now, I promise."

His lips smiled around his finger, even as around his eyes there were little winces. "I sorta like it." He jiggled some more, his chin shining.

"Come on, Raymond, it's for your own good."

He required a lot of convincing, but eventually I persuaded him to come upstairs and let Doctor Judy try. (I thought: if only my mother could see me now!) Raymond was going to get the kind of sistering he deserved.

With a steady stream of talk I kept him distracted while I tied the string to the doorknob. He stepped up to the threshhold with his mouth open. "Wider," I kept telling him, "wider!" Looking in there. He was cavernous.

Suddenly, a strange idea popped into my mind. I swear I didn't plan it. At first the idea alone seemed enough—funny, in a way—but then, as if to prove I could really do it, I looped the string around an adjacent, perfectly good tooth.

Unsuspecting, he blinked at me over his cheekbones. Waiting.

My insides felt tight. Maybe I would've done the right thing and taken the string off, but I felt foolish and embarrassed to have put myself in this situation; a part of me was waiting, Oh what now? I panicked.

I reached out and slammed the door with all my might.

Oh, the blood that streamed out afterward!

47

"Close your mouth! Close your mouth!"

"Juthy, I arf—"

"No—please!"

A very dirty trick, I admit. Immediately I regretted it, and hadn't the slightest desire to laugh. In fact, as I watched him reel then stumble toward me, I wanted to scream. His lips clamped together and he choked, blood spurted out of the corners of his mouth.

"Raymond, no!" I grabbed him by the arm. "Come on, come!" We pounded down the stairs; in the kitchen he peeled up his shirt to the bleeding, blotting his face. "It's going to be all right," I told him, "it's nothing, you'll see, you'll see." Eventually we stanched the flow with wadded-up paper towels.

At least half an hour passed before he realized the truth. By then my parents had come home, and I'd taken care of most of the mess, except what my mother found on the stairs. Raymond was seething.

"You stupidhead!" he said—then quickly reinserted a washcloth in his mouth.

"Judy, I can't believe you don't know better!" she said.

"I'm sorry, I'm sorry!" I shouted. "But all his pointed teeth look alike!"

No one even suspected that it wasn't an accident. They just assumed I was dumb. In fact my father said out loud I was brainless.

"He bled on me, too! He bled on me."

I didn't know how to defend myself, and most of all wanted someone to feel sorry for me. It wasn't easy being so bad. Heaven had never seemed so far away.

"That's enough, enough!" he barked. Not a grain of sympathy. "Get out of my sight."

That day was Extra Big Trouble, for usually I could count on my father to take my side since Raymond's crying reminded him of Uncle Rod back when he was a kid. It got on his nerves. More than once he'd eyed

Raymond, shaking his head, saying, "Son, try not to be a pure pain in the ass." But this time he told me to simmer down, saying that my smart mouth reminded him of Uncle Rod and he'd make me sorry if I didn't shut my jaw. My father seemed uninterested by how much I loved my brother, or my brother loved me. From then on he began to hold his head in his hands more often, saying he just wanted some peace.

5

My Prayer

So maybe I was hungry for an example; figuring out life and death in the shadow of the Seymour water tower was too much for me, and never mind fancy explanations. What I wanted were clear instructions like what was written on the side of a box of pancake mix. *First, empty contents into a deep receptacle. . .*

One sticky July evening a long blue car coasted into our driveway. It was dusty, the front grill spattered with dead butterflies. The engine revved, then died—the horn tooted twice. Uncle Rod got out of the car, wearily, then bent over and reached inside. The back of his shirt was soaked with sweat. When he turned around, in his arms was the biggest watermelon I'd ever seen. Striped like a tiger.

He saw me standing at the edge of the garden beside a row of fat-headed hyacinths. I'd been talking to them, egging them on to grow even more. This was scientific. "Come on, that's very good but don't stop now. Please take my advice. Go! Live! Grow!" I'd planted the bulbs myself. From the end of the driveway, my uncle's voice reached me:

> *Yeah, it's Big Rod*
> *By God!*
> *Let it rain*
> *Like a tall dog!*

I looked at the sky. Not a cloud.

My father, who was scraping the side of the house with a putty knife, scooted down the ladder with surprising speed. Smiling, paint chips in his hair, he seemed genuinely pleased to see my uncle. My mother shouted hello through a basement screen, where she was washing with a rag around the window frame.

It had been three years. We went out back to the picnic table and all of a sudden it was like a party, the profound *thwup* as my father's big carving knife split the melon in half: the red flesh and shining black seeds jumped into sight. My mother laughed, told Uncle Rod he hadn't changed a bit, but I could see his face had become softer. His sideburns were long, and grew broader at their ends. He looked at me and I was shy, had nothing to say to him.

"Are you the same, Judy?" he asked. "Are you?"

I shrugged, made no answer. What a question. I was taller, anybody could see. Getting stringy, my father said.

Their voices rose higher, excited, exchanging exclamations. "We weren't expecting you!" and "Where's your suntan?" and "The ground's still moving under me!" Uncle Rod announced he'd driven twenty six hours nonstop, his butt was asleep, full of pins. My father said he hated that, just hated it. Lots of black coffee was the only remedy. My mother said there was potato salad. The sun was going down behind a neighbor's house and seemed very close, intense; as I listened to them and watched the rays filter over the roof, one striking my mother and turning her skin a honey gold as she tugged at the gauze wrapping around her thumb which she'd cut terribly near the bone making the potato salad, suddenly I heard my uncle's question again, in my head: *"Are you the same?"* Maybe he wasn't talking about the fact that I was taller, maybe he was talking about something else. After all, I *felt* the same, inside.

It was true. He was the same inside, too—I could tell by his voice. Did people really change? I wondered. Was everybody like Rod and me?

My father was in such good spirits that he took Uncle Rod over to see the filled-in dinosaur hole. For over a year after Rod and I had dug it, the hole had remained in our backyard, wide open. My father refused to touch it. He said that it wasn't his folly. My parents had arguments about this, my mother replying that in any case it was an eyesore, a danger. A yawning pit— why, Raymond could fall in it! (When I giggled, they looked at me strangely.) How could we allow such a hazard?

"Oh, good gravy," he said. "Everybody knows to keep clear of it."

"But Raymond doesn't! That's exactly the point!"

This was because Raymond liked the hole. It was one of his distractions. He would pick up his cat, walk up to the edge, and toss the cat down inside. With a leap and scrabbling flurry, the cat would climb its way out. Then Raymond followed the cat around the yard and under bush until he could catch it again, and drop it in the hole; the cat would scrabble; and on and on. It would be an exaggeration to say that the cat enjoyed this procedure as much as Raymond did, but we'd gotten it as a kitten, so it had never known another life. It was a sickly, shedding orange creature that understood only how to lick itself. After a time the game became a maddening thing to witness, for it was always the same, the cat going limp, yellow eyes turning up at the sky, Raymond caressing it, saying softly, "There's the hole, Charlie, there, Charlie," (Raymond released his grip), "there—"

And down.

But my father wouldn't listen to my mother. No, as a matter of principle he would not fill this hole. His brother had agreed to repair it, so he was waiting for Rod to make good on his promise. (My uncle had always said the day of the dinosaur bone had got blown out of proportion; there was no need to get upset about something so easy to fix.) Yet somehow Rod never got around to it. Then he wore his leather pants, and was off to Florida: it appeared we would have the hole forever. It gaped in the backyard and from time to time reminded me of him. I was the only one in the family who made an effort to take care of it, removing leaves and debris with the change of seasons.

One day, however, our neighbor Kevin Barton ran across our yard after a baseball and in his dull unimaginative way (I saw it—to this day I am not convinced he didn't do it on purpose) tumbled in headfirst. He put his hands before him to catch himself, and promptly broke both his wrists. We had to pull him out by his feet.

This changed everything. My father was scared out of his wits that he was going to be sued by Ralph Barton, a retreaded tire salesman whom he considered ruthless, and my father panicked. Late that night in the pitch black he went out to the backyard and filled the hole, principle or no principle; he coached my mother and me to say "Hole? What hole?" until my mother began to cry. For over a week he was in a state of great anxiety, and very bitter.

"It's unfair!" he said. "You try all your life not to make any trouble—you're honest, do your best—and look what you end up with."

"You're taking it too personal," my mother told him.

"Well, I've been snookered! That's what it comes down to, living with this so near, and there's nothing anybody can say or do."

"Don't say that!"

In fact we weren't sued, though my father discovered that he was missing his pine watch that he'd been given as the lumberyard's Employee of the Year. My mother suspected he'd lost it in the back yard the night when he was working frantically in the dark. My parents argued about whether he should try to dig it up. Was the watch really down there? Would it still be ticking? Sometimes my father could be seen in the backyard standing on the spot, looking down at his feet, cussing.

But now he took Uncle Rod to visit the filled-in hole, and my uncle lit a cigarette, remarked what a nice job he had done. Uncle Rod exhaled smoke through his nostrils, said how mighty good it felt to be back, too. No sir, he didn't regret leaving his life down there, delivering beehives. He asked about Grandpa, who was living alone now, and beginning to forget; had Grandpa received the hairy coconut he'd mailed him on his birthday, just for chuckles? Then we went back to sit at the picnic table, where he told us some of his jokes without punch lines. "How many rabbits does it take?"; and, "Why do blind men write graffiti at the bottom of the ocean?" My father smiled. I sank my teeth into a juicy half-moon of melon.

We had a competition to see who could spit a seed the farthest, and Raymond got a spanking. A little later, in the twilight when my mother sent me back to the house to get newspapers for the rinds, my father's attitude changed. I came back to the picnic table and my father was asking: "But for how long, Rod? Sure we can put you up but for how long?" My mother rose to her feet, wiping her fingers one by one on a tissue, staring at my father, but my father wouldn't look at her. Uncle Rod shrugged. "Not long. Just till I get established again."

That was a wonderful summer. My uncle made a room for himself up in the attic, rolled down a raffia rug and installed fans. He also helped my father repaint the house. It was hard to believe what a huge difference a creamy new paint job made. You thought: the people who live in that house must be smart-looking, too. So I tried to be. That summer my appearance began to matter to me. I had a pair of tan cotton slacks that tied with a string at the side—very stylish, I thought—the kind intended for holiday lounging. You couldn't get them off me. Shorts seemed so, so—ordinary. And though my mother sometimes railed about my appearance, declared she got hot just looking at me and for heaven's sake why didn't I cut my hair or at least put it up in braids like other summers (as she said this, sweat trickled in a slant along her collarbone and down between her breasts, for the sight of me seemed to increase her temperature by ten degrees: "Do something, Judy, please, I'm cooking in my own juices!")—I did not relent. We snapped beans together; her words floated past . . . . Oh, how I wished my family made more of an effort for their appearance! Everyone, everything around me was ready for fixing up.

The inside of our house was a nightmare. There was the depressing laundry pile that never seemed to get any smaller (even if people dressed like pigs, I noticed, they sure used up a lot of laundry); and there were the openings my father had cut in the ceiling for heat to pass through in winter, where in all seasons Raymond liked to stick his stupid face, or drop Charlie through, when Charlie was indoors (I hated those openings, they were so stressful); and worst of all was the way my father had rigged the bathroom. Though he worked at the lumberyard, he wasn't what you called handy. The toilet, an ancient porcelain monster shaped like a bone in your ear, you had to jiggle—not the handle, but the whole toilet. This required a certain amount of strength. I did it for Raymond, one of my fun jobs. He was scared of it. *Finally* we replaced it when Grandpa threw out his back one Sunday after he'd joined us for dinner. He came out of the bathroom, all white, completely bent over.

"Cramps, Dad?" my father said.

"You just go to hell," my grandfather replied.

Rod was lucky. He could escape. At any hour of the

day or night he might hop into his long blue Polara that my father said he ran the piss out of, and *leave*. How I envied him that. Probably my first lesson in social mobility!

"Can I go with you?" I begged, and depending on the hour, or sometimes, whether a warm, preoccupied look shone in his eyes (on these occasions I didn't stand a chance), he might say yes. Might. He kept his car in the shade of the pin oak tree where it appeared poised for action, faithful as a steed, shadows of leaves dappling the windshield. On one side toward the rear the gas cap was missing, and a rag was stuffed in its place. Somehow my eyes always went straight to the rag; there was something distracting about it. One day I was passing by and pulled it out—a pair of woman's panties. For a moment I froze, staring at what was in my hand. "Wha—?" Hastily I stuffed the panties back, and looked around, in case anyone had seen me.

When Uncle Rod was around the house, he kept Raymond occupied, started him collecting buffalo nickels, which he planted in pocket change and hid in obvious places around the yard till Raymond acquired the mistaken impression that the buffaloes were not scarce. *"Put your ear to the ground, bub, listen . . .hey, what's that by your nose?"* My disputes with Raymond were less frequent because he was old enough now to appreciate the force of words of those wiser, though once when I was advising him he lost his cool and punched me in the kidney. This hurt in the most amazing way, as if suddenly a wasps' nest had split open in my side, and in the middle of a sentence I found myself on the floor, my cheek grinding into the living room rug. I doubt Raymond was trying to fight extra vicious that day, it was only, as he claimed afterward, because he was shorter and couldn't reach higher, but my uncle pulled him aside and told him it was dirty boxing, and if I needed a transplant, the doctors would come looking for *him.* How my brother's expression changed when he heard this! He went off to a corner and started chewing his lips.

Yet that day amounted to little in comparison with the lasting shock of an afternoon in July when I was out on the back stoop with Charlie the cat, speaking to him and sort of laughing to myself, for Charlie's mouth hung open, his head bobbed so it looked as if he were talking back—we were having a conversation, Charlie and I—when suddenly out of his mouth dropped a fat, copper-colored worm. Fell wiggling and rolling over, convulsing radially from shiny tip to shiny tip, just one inch from my hand. I screamed, ran into the house, told everybody, who hurried out in time to see Charlie shitting a stream of them on the grass. Terrible! Raymond's eyes grew wide, but he didn't cry. He started telling Charlie in a soft voice to stop it. "Hang on, okay? Take my advice. Just stop."

Over the next few hours Charlie did not stop; they kept coming and coming; my uncle's voice carried up to me from the yard through the window of my upstairs bedroom where I was trying to hide away, his announcement to my parents that it was perhaps the worst case of worms in history. Though my mother took Charlie to the vet, who stuck him with needles (my father was afraid to take him), it was too late. He lasted only one more day, producing ever more evidence of this worst case before shivering to death in the rose bushes.

We were all shaken up, and afterward his importance grew in our eyes, somehow. "He was an all-right cat," my father went as far as to say, "not one of those half-assed ones." My uncle nodded, his hand unsteady as he lit a cigarette. "Imagine that: coming after you while you're still alive." I tried and tried to throw off the first image of talking Charlie and from then on was unable, against all reason, to speak to a cat again, while Raymond took to playing by himself and could be seen sprinting up and down the back alley, arms churning. A fast runner for his age, he pretended he was one of those long black men on TV. My mother smiled as he flashed by the gap where our gate was supposed to be, but I knew better. Raymond believed that if he ran fast enough, he would disappear.

Aside from horror, though, most of summer was a season of grace, respecting a rhythm of its own. Sleepy mornings with heat already buzzing in the windows, a few birds wheezing on the other side of the screen and maybe an occasional *bang!* as next door Ralph Barton threw used cans of spray paint into his incinerator. Blessed, he never got hurt. Lunch was fat ripe tomatoes from the garden, their red and yellow skins stretched tight to splitting. In the afternoon time slowed conspicuously—two hours might take three—and Uncle Rod drove me and my girlfriends to the swimming pool in his long blue Polara.

While we swam, Rod parked in the shade of a nearby picnic area where he studied short fat books of baseball statistics and listened to day games on the radio. At any moment I might pull myself out of the pool, run up to the chain link fence with water streaming down my back and legs. "Uncle! Hey Uncle!"

He looked up, smiling.

I pranced before the fence, for the concrete burned under my feet, even as a sudden breeze gave me goosebumps everywhere else. "Why doncha swim?" I called, sweeping wet hair off my face. "Come in with us!"

He shook his head.

"Naw. That chlorine wrecks your sinuses. You be careful, Judy."

I turned around, still doing my dance, then ran to the edge of the water, leaped: a delicious belly-smacking pop.

My uncle had found a part-time job back at the Van Allen School of Mortuary Science, though not what he wanted; that summer they took him on as a night janitor. He accepted it as a temporary measure. He also found time to take me and my friends one Saturday to the drive-in theatre to see an all-night showing of every *Planet of the Apes* movie ever made. Ten hours of non-stop entertainment! He bought us whatever we wanted at the concession stand, talked along at the screen, kept us giggling all night. At one point he rolled up his sleeve to show us the tattoo on his arm:

BIG ROD

et

MADELEINE

pour toujours

His skin looked yellow in the car light, the tattoo ink was a sad, squiggly blue; then he clicked his door shut and we couldn't see anymore. I felt proud in front of my friends, yet a little jealous, too, for he hadn't shown me the tattoo before.

"Gee, Big Rod, what's it mean?" asked my friend Kim from the backseat. She was always trying to sit next to Rod, but I saw to it that she didn't. "Pore-too-jewers? What's it mean?"

"It means forever," he said softly, buttoning his cuff. "That's what it means. Forever."

There was a hush in the car, just music crackling through the speaker in our window, then suddenly Uncle Rod let out a laugh: "Hanh-hanh-hanh-hanh." We jumped—it was scary, this laugh. Like the sound I'd heard him make up in his room when he had severe sinus pain. He drummed the steering wheel with his fist, honking once, and the people in the car in front of us turned around, while above on the screen a swarming mob of angry apes climbed over a wall. Everyone in our car joined in laughing, except me.

The next day my parents made me go to church while Uncle Rod slept all morning on his bed in the attic. It was painful to be shaken awake at nine o'clock to get dressed, but my mother and father left me no choice. This Sunday I was *so, so tired*. I could hardly keep my eyes open.

During the service I prayed for Uncle Rod, for him to have a family and live as happily as the rest of us. Happy . . . happy . . . . At one point I realized my prayer was rambling, I was drifting off, and with tremendous effort forced my eyes open. Blinking, with stinging eyes, I was sure for an instant everyone in the pews looked like apes. I swear. But my prayer was sincere.

6

The Need for Forgiveness

Uncle Rod lived with us for two years. I got used to having him around the house, though in time my mother's opinion of him began to color my own. My uncle spoke of many plans—of moving out West, or up north to the Michigan Peninsula to farm civet cats, for perfume, or to the outskirts of our town and starting a nursery for bonsai trees (this was before anybody had heard of them—actually, Uncle Rod *did* have some winning ideas). What about, he speculated, buying a piece of the Tulip Lanes, a mainly Dutch bowling alley? It was up for grabs.

But none of these plans ever came to fruition. He stayed on as part-time night janitor at the Van Allen School. The only thing you could be sure about Uncle Rod, my mother muttered under her breath, was that he would never miss a meal.

How he loved to eat! Stacks of syrup-gooey pancakes with little turdy sausages in the morning; bumpy dill gherkins with cheese between slices of bread slathered with his favorite seedy brown mustard, so potent it brought tears to my eyes, at noon; and in the evening two or three tangled heaps of spaghetti, with buttered garlic toast and red bean salad on the side, followed by cookies and vanilla ice cream with bananas and cracked walnuts on top, for dessert.

"Taste this," he ordered, thrusting a parsleyed beet or a baby new potato with peppercorns in your face. "Is this sensational or what?" His enjoyment depended in no small part on someone else sharing the experience. You felt selfish not to, and often his offerings were, in fact, a pleasure, though you might spend the rest of the afternoon discreetly shielding your mouth with your hand to direct hot silent belches.

Yet if a meal were small, if we tried to economize a bit, he never complained. In those days before my uncle acquired wealth, he didn't *expect* a big spread. As long as he had plenty of bread and his mustard, maybe a (crunchy, never mealy) apple, he was satisfied. When we had chicken he always volunteered to eat the skin. In the summer he could consume a three-gallon bucket of Boston lettuce in one day; our garden had always produced more lettuce than we could keep up with, till he moved in. If my grandfather happened to be around he said it was a pitiful sight to see, for you might as well watch a man eat a bale of hay. "You'd think he wanted to be a fatted calf only he don't look like a fatted calf— what's eatin' him inside?" Inevitably Grandpa and Rod would get into an argument, about anything, as long as they could argue. They tackled all subjects: Our Lizard-faced President or Daylight Saving Time or the debatable merits of neapolitan in a carton. Many wasted words, and at any rate our lettuce cost us almost nothing, like our tomatoes: during tomato season Uncle Rod ate them till his mouth was filled with sores.

Before dinner, he often took his seat at the table early and during our preparations read the newspaper aloud and informed us what was going on in the world. Planes fell out of the sky, a new species of wild goat was discovered in the forests of Thailand, a man locked himself in his own car trunk for forty three hours. "Look at this—Goddamn," he exclaimed one evening while I was putting out the plates. His head suddenly bobbed above the pages. "It says here that if you consider the whole planet, the entire population, there's somebody dying every One point Seven Five seconds. Now how about that?" Silence. After a moment he cleared his throat, looked around and continued: "What's interesting, you see, is that that's almost exactly the same as a person's respiration. Of course they leave that out. But put the two together, see what you get: every breath you take, somebody dies. Imagine."

"That's great, Rod," my father said, "cheer us up, for crying out loud." He pulled a handkerchief from his pocket and rubbed the windowpane, squeaking, then squinted at the rain gauge he'd attached to the side of the house. My father wanted to be able to monitor the moisture without going outside and getting his shoes wet, and with this new gauge he would watch from a position of dry comfort, even at night, by the light of his window. Precipitation in progress—he would miss none of the drama. Unfortunately, though, his initial idea hadn't taken into account the overhang of the roof, so in order to get a measurement he'd had to fix the gauge on a plank extending several feet away from the sill, which had the consequence of making the gauge extremely difficult to read: all those little gradations of tenths of inches. He squinched his eyebrows into knots, trying to make out the numbers. Drove himself crazy. Now he swore under his breath and turned to my uncle, said, "There's nothing you can do about death, fella. The world turns. We got either two tenths or four tenths here, I can't tell. Or maybe it's in between, three tenths. Depends on the angle."

"Will you quit looking at that thing?" my mother said, breaking off thin arms of celery. "You never see it the same way twice."

"I think they lie on TV," my father said. "This is proof."

"Every breath I take, somebody dies." Uncle Rod inhaled. "There goes one now." When he looked at me I froze, clutching plates to my stomach. Involuntarily I

65

held my breath, and kept holding it even after he exhaled, then breathed again. "There's another!" he announced. His chest moved in, out. "Another!"

"That's not funny," my mother said.

"I'm not saying it is! I wish I knew how to make it different. Every breath I take, the madder I get."

My father frowned. "That's no way to live. A person's gotta come to terms."

I felt myself turning red.

"Why?" my uncle said, and with two mighty shakes folded up the newspaper pages. He had an impressive way of making them crash. "Why humor death? You have to put your foot down somewhere, if you ask me. No thank you."

My mother flicked on a burner on the stove. "It's true that facing up to the inevitable requires a bit of *effort*."

"Annie, that has nothing to do with it. What people call 'coming to terms' is just pooching out, really. It's no answer, it's an attitude, and a dumb one at that. Like telling a guy if he smiles, that's enough to make him happy. Or somebody lying in bed sick with a temperature, if only he'd jump out and do fifty push-ups, he'd feel better."

My mother tapped a wooden spoon on the lip of a pan. "There's no choice involved, Mister. A person has to accept death. It's part of life."

"Right, right, I hear that one a lot. You mean, like if you eat, you're gonna shit, too? You can't have one without the other? But let's not confuse the two! The way you say it, it's like you don't allow yourself to act on the difference. It's like telling a person to eat shit. That's not a nice thing to say, Annie."

My mother turned around, open-mouthed, but before she could reply, air burst from my cheeks, "pbrrrrr!"

"Judy!"

"I'm sorry," I gasped. "I didn't do it on purpose."

"Somebody else just dropped," Rod said.

I took in fast breaths, and Rod added, "there goes someone else, and someone else, and someone else."

"Is this some kind of game between you two?" my mother demanded. "This is sick."

"What about heaven?" I asked him, my voice coming out high. "You forget that!"

He wrinkled his face for a moment, then reached for his newspaper again, began to unfold it. "Aw, I guess I shouldn't've brought this up. Everybody's so damn touchy. Sorry folks, never mind."

"Hold on, brother," my father said. He'd begun to spread cream cheese into celery stalks, and now pointed one at my uncle. "Why doncha answer her?"

Rod sighed. (In spite of myself, I thought: there goes *another*.) "Oh, holy moly," he said. "You got me walking on rotten eggs. You don't really want to hear it." He stopped, but we stared at him, waiting. Eventually he continued, "Not everybody goes to heaven, right? A lot of people don't make it, right?"

We nodded.

"So is that really a *comfort* to you? First Annie says to eat shit, then you tell people—tell me—to go to hell. Why, is that a decent way to talk?"

My mother stepped forward, grabbed the back of a chair, leaned toward him. "You twist everything around, just everything! The way you talk. I won't go along with it, I won't! It's more than vulgar. Worse! What if everybody thought like you? What if everybody acted like you?" She swung one of her chapped hands in the air. "What would get done?"

Rod didn't raise his voice. He reached over to the plate for a piece of celery, not looking at us; with his finger he smoothed cream cheese along the celery's ridge. (Sometimes my father's lack of neatness stressed him.) He licked his finger, then bit with a crunch. "I'm not asking anybody to think like me. I don't expect anybody to act like me. When did you ever hear me say that? I suppose everyone'd be happier if they thought like themselves. They should act like themselves." His voice grew softer. "Isn't it more, really, that you want me to act like you?"

She lifted the chair several inches, then brought it down with a bump. "There—there you go! Twisting it again!"

And this time, my father took her side.

"You can think whatever you damn please, Rod. But that don't mean you can't get a job."

"I got a job, Carl!"

"I mean—I mean something full-time. Why, a guy like you could have a career. Sure you're gonna die but so's everybody else, we all are, so we might as well work more, you see?" My father wrinkled his brow. "Let me try that again."

Turning away from him, Rod faced me with saddening eyes.

"You could try it as a sports announcer," my father went on. "You're a natural. Why not give it a shot?" At this Rod sighed again (and another person expired— how, I wondered, was he happy, usually merrier than the rest of us, if he thought as he claimed, and got madder with each breath? How?). He didn't answer my father. That night he left the table early, without dessert, which had never happened before. Mulberry sauce, too! It was downright eerie.

My father had been dead serious about my uncle trying a career as a sports announcer. For this, unlike the plans for the bowling alley or civet cats, he was ready to help Rod, for he fervently believed in his brother's talent. During the Saturday Game of the Week he would turn down the volume of the TV and let Uncle Rod call the action. And it was true, Rod was very good—he knew all the players and their records, could instantly tell you whether they were right- or left-handed, even their hometown, and whether they were married. "Chuck is the pride of Williston, Mon-TAN-ah," Rod would intone, "the big red-headed kid—look at those freckles!—led all third basemen in put-outs the year before last, and this babyface still finds time to teach gun safety." I didn't give a hoot about baseball, couldn't care less who won or lost, but if Uncle Rod happened to be calling the game as I walked by the room, I found myself pausing to listen; a minute later, I might sit down to join them. He pitched his voice higher than usual, the words came faster, and with this headlong delivery it was no longer just a silly game where men with big butts and black smudges under their eyes swatted at a little ball— no, it was a spectacle, with real characters now, such as the outfielder christened Wally "No Knees" because of his six operations, a washed-up slugger in desperate need of a hit or he'd soon be out of a job—oh, the pain on his face! Or a quick little strutting Georgian you could always count on to try and steal second: *there he goes!* I could believe my father, maybe Uncle Rod could've made it as an announcer. He could really be somebody. He would have accomplishments he could write back to Albert Livingstone, who according to last year's card, was now dean of a woman's college in Oregon.

But Uncle Rod always tired after a couple of innings and turned up the TV's volume. "Don't," my father said, "keep on!"

"No, that's enough," said Uncle Rod, settling back in his seat. "Let's not overdo it. There's always room for more in your own head if you like."

And they would go on watching. The TV announcers' voices droned, the instant replay unfurled, but now it all seemed useless. My father would take a long, shiny nail out of his pocket and use its head to clean his ears, with a look of soporific, drugged-out bliss. He and my uncle sat there for hours, getting up only during commercials to go to the bathroom and becoming grouchy if there were a rain delay.

My mother worked all day Saturdays at the supermarket so there was only me to take care of them, feed them, bring them beer. (Beer was good for mouth sores, Uncle Rod said, though when I sneaked a taste of the stuff in the kitchen I thought it was awful—eeeesh, they had to be stupid.) At first my father hadn't liked the idea of my mother taking a job outside the home, but when it came down to it, with the new shag rug and twin recliners in the living room and the new ceiling tiles in my parents' bedroom, we needed the money. After the first three months, she started working full-time. My uncle helped out some around the house; he liked to hoe in the garden, evenings when it was cool, and wash and wax and polish the cars, and he kept the birdbath full, but that wasn't much, really. He wasn't getting fat like my father—he looked as if he could do a lot more. Especially those sunny days when he stretched himself full-length on the picnic table, hands folded behind his head as he gazed at the sky. I remember him laughing. What was he laughing at?

One Saturday afternoon during the Game of the Week while I was doing the lunch dishes there was a knock at the door. The back door, which was strange. At first I thought it was Raymond and Monty fooling around. (Raymond had a new Best Friend now, a muscle-shirted boy who was skinny to the point of being translucent, who called me Nudie instead of Judy— that's how witty he was—who was always goosing my brother or burning his mouth with cinnamon toothpicks.) I ignored the knock at first. But the knock sounded again, so I wiped off my hands and opened, expecting their squeals of laughter.

Instead there was a woman with streaky blonde hair. She was very pale. She said Big Rod Gass lived here, didn't he? The woman had a different accent, she said "Rawd." I asked her to come in.

70

I showed her to the living room, where Uncle Rod was saying, "Is it possible that Manny, the clutch maestro, is the best pinch hitter in the history of the game? Really?—" then stopped. He looked at us. The blonde woman's face twisted, then all at once caved in. She was crying. Uncle Rod sprang up. The woman turned and ran out of the room, almost knocked me over. The kitchen door slammed. My uncle stood in the middle of the floor, saying "*Jesus. Jesus.*"

"What's—what's going on?" asked my father, rolling, squeaking in his chair.

"Fuck," said Uncle Rod.

I was astonished. This was the first time the word was ever uttered in our house. At this moment it was more than unexpected, it also seemed a development, like sending a monkey into outer space. Was it really possible? I was only about fourteen and though I'd heard my father use plenty of bad words, there was never That One—That One existed apart. The whole house seemed for an instant unsteady on its foundations and we stood frozen as if waiting for everything to crumble around us.

The back door slammed *again*. And she was back, with a long blond toddler with red blotches on his face. He squirmed in her arms.

"Little Rod," said my uncle.

She began screaming at him, and he started shouting back; my father walked around them, trying to put in a word, but from the beginning he was totally irrelevant and overwhelmed—actually staggering. She kept saying "Don't lie to me, Rawd, don't you lie!" Her thin arm flailed the air. Little Rod began to bawl, and choke. "Stop it, Beth, stop it!" shouted my uncle. I watched, wide-eyed. It all had something to do with money. She wanted $900, right now. She wanted her $900. He said it was coming, it was coming, he'd never intended not to pay her. "Liar!" she hissed, "liar!" letting little Rod slide down her side where he clung to her leg, so that when

71

she took a step forward in the excitement she dragged him like a clubfoot. "Please," my father was saying, "p-p-please." But he sounded four miles away.

Eventually Uncle Rod and Beth eased off, lowered their voices; there was no more shouting or waving of arms. "What am I supposed to do?" she sobbed. "I don't know anymore." Rod announced that he preferred to discuss this affair in private.

Beth sniffled, wiped her face with the heel of her hand, looked at my father and me then agreed, yes, this was private. So she and my uncle went up to his room in the attic, while Little Rod stayed with us. She wasn't going to leave him strapped out in the car, she declared. "Excuse us," she said.

Now my father didn't look at me. He stared at the TV screen, his face clouding, then he swore. He got up and turned on the sound.

"No one ever tells me anything!" I blurted, but he didn't answer. I was fuming. Little Rod cowered at the other end of the couch, eating a Daffy-Taffy his mother had offered to pacify him, along with the promise that she'd be right back. He'd like the nice girl, Beth said. (Me!) She didn't even ask my name. To my surprise, Little Rod didn't kick up another fuss. He curled his legs under him and watched us (in seconds he managed to have a sticky face) while my father wouldn't so much as cast a glance in our direction. My temples pounded. God oh God, I was furious.

"They married?" I asked.

My father was silent.

"I said ARE THEY MARRIED?"

My father grunted, in a way that I took to mean Yes, though I could've been wrong. Maybe the grunt meant they *had* been married, but were no more. I waited for further explanation but almost a minute dragged by with my father using his long, shiny nail, impassive, while Little Rod licked and stickied himself even more. I wasn't stupid. I knew that Uncle Rod had already been married once a long time ago. And that there were nights when he didn't come home now, back to his attic roost. It seemed pretty obvious to me, pretty simple: my uncle was not living up to his responsibilities. He was cheating people. *He was a bad man.* I should detest him for this, I thought. Why should he receive special consideration? Why should he be immune from obligation? Yes, I should detest him for this. With gritted teeth, I pictured Beth. I had no proof . . . but I felt a queasy certainty. *I knew whose panties those had been in his gas tank!*

I detested my father, too. Somehow he shared the blame. We sat in silence, except for the baseball babble on TV, and I thought of every bad thing I could muster, of my mother saying Uncle Rod was lazy. Yes, it was true. Goldbrick! Do-nothing! A sit around, kicked-back loafer!

I thought too of The Word he had uttered in our house. You could still feel the echoes. "What are they doing up there?" I asked, and now my father turned his head, told me to Shut Up.

This came like a slap. I was stunned. Oh, how *ugly*! I resolved never to speak to my father again!

"Get me something to eat," he mumbled. "Soda crackers and peanut butter."

Trembling, I got up. Pig! I thought, my fingers clenching into fists. PIG! There would come a day when I had my own house, and took no orders!

My uncle and Beth were up in the attic for three whole innings. Little Rod whimpered from time to time, but generally stared at the TV. My father didn't even offer to change channels for him. I wanted to shake the man, slap him, for real. He deserved it. He made smacking sounds like a dog when the peanut butter stuck to the roof of his mouth.

When Uncle Rod and Beth came down they were

very quiet, and respectful with each other. Only my father got a little agitated—but he wrote a check for $500, signing his name with a mighty rip. Then Beth and little Rod went back to their car. My father grabbed me by the arm and pulled me outside to wave. My uncle leaned into the car and kissed little Rod's blotchy cheeks. Beth began to cry again, her face twisting up, her hair in her eyes; I don't know how she could see to drive. The car with its "See Florida" plates bounced into the street.

My father stood scowling, in one of his silent rages, and when he stopped waving, tromped back into the house and slammed the door. Uncle Rod was coming up the sidewalk, and I thought it was a good thing my mother wasn't here to see this, a good thing. (Yet I wished she could, too.) I barked at him.

"Why don't you take care of your little boy?"

"I do," he said softly.

"No you don't! No you don't!"

"I would," he said firmly. Now he was beside me, face to face.

"Why don't you? Why?"

"They wouldn't let me."

"Who wouldn't let you? Who's stopping you?"

"Everybody. She is. Your folks are. The judge. Everybody."

"I don't believe you. I—I don't understand. No, I don't believe you."

His calm flustered me. He looked away, down the street.

"I've always said I would take him. I would raise him. I'd be glad to."

"Then why don't you?"

"That's a good question."

"I hate you. I hate you."

It was out before I knew what I was saying. The words hurt him, I could see. He brought up a hand quickly to his shoulder, then let it fall again. Yet I wasn't sorry. I was glad to have hurt him.

"It's a good question," he said, "because they won't give me an answer. I swear, Judy: I would take him tomorrow. His mother, no, but him, yes. But I tell you they won't let me. I would raise him the way I want to."

"Where? Here?"

"Why not?" he said. "Why not? How can you criticize me for not doing something, when you won't let me do it? Why not?"

"But—there's not just you. There's Mom and Dad. And Raymond. There's, there's me," I said, and felt myself strangling.

"Yes. And I'm disappointed in you, Judy," he said, and left me, went in the house. Somehow this, this, even through all my anger, wounded me worst of all, and I grabbed at my hair, wanting to tell him from the moment he turned his back that I was sorry. Even through my hatred, I wanted his forgiveness.

7

Hardball

Uncle Rod moved out shortly after Beth's visit. He acted in a hurry, swallowing his words as he packed his affairs and rolled up his raffia rug, took his witch hazel from the bathroom and his boots and kit from the hall closet. Upon leaving he gave my mother a gift: a ruby ring. My mother was surprised, even a little embarrassed, but she softened toward him after this. She said for my uncle there was maybe "the benefit of the doubt." Not that her esteem was subject to barter—her heart was too full of both generosity and resentment, for that—but the gesture meant something to her, an acknowledgment on his part, giving some credit where it was due. His suitcase in the trunk of his Polara, a sad smile on his face, Uncle Rod told her, "You know, Annie, the trouble with people is that they're human." He held out a tiny package. "It's a handicap they can never overcome."

My mother accepted the ring, put it on, lifting her hand to capture the light. Its stone was as big as a cough drop. "Thanks, Rod," she said shyly. Thereafter she never took the ring off, and on the whole adopted a more live-and-let-live attitude toward my uncle. Especially now that he would live somewhere else.

For me, though, a barrier existed. This lasted long after Beth's visit and Rod's hasty departure. Perhaps because my expectations for my uncle had been higher. Perhaps because for me, it was a question of love—and God damn him, look what he'd done. It was a terrible thing to learn, that my love could be trifled with. During my high school days I could admire my uncle only at a distance: the man in my mind, who with each passing year resembled more and more the Corporal Roderick H. Gass of the black-and-white Army portrait, the young soldier with the sweet face and knowing eyes—not the Uncle Rod with creases in his cheeks who lived in a cramped furnished room piled high with old baseball magazines above a dry cleaners downtown, with a traffic light flashing next to his window. The glowing colors leaked into the room even when he pulled the shade. Green: yellow: red. "Drove me nuts at first," he said, waving his arm at the colors, "but a person gets used to it." His favorite stunt for visitors was to obey the lights. Suddenly he would stop talking, perhaps in the middle of a sentence, or stop walking in the center of the room—frozen—and you noticed the room was aglow with red. When it turned yellow, he would begin to smile. And when it turned green, he started moving again, tossed back his head and laughed, Henc-henc-henc-henc, mouth open wide and showing you the tobacco stains on his teeth: in the room directly above someone flushed the toilet: the pipes on the wall clunked. Henc-henc.

He was still a part-time janitor at the Van Allen School of Mortuary Science, and never expressed a desire to earn a living elsewhere. Despite his allergy to constructive purpose, he was not a drunk nor hamstrung by depression: you had to admit he avoided the common traps. Most of the time he seemed satisfied, even busy. He took up card tricks, and sedulously discussing with Jehovah's Witnesses and assorted evangelicals who rang his bell until all their arguments were used up and they were speechless, exhausted, even rude, getting up to leave while he was still talking, and pulling the door closed in my uncle's face.

He adopted a pair of flaming parakeets, counted himself a success at celebrating when necessary or offering a yarn, and more than anyone I knew, seriously listened to the radio. He preferred to get his baseball action from disembodied airwaves, and watched TV contests only to humor my father. Sometimes he called the games on the radio, too, just as he did for TV. He turned down the volume and would talk aloud an inning or two, and then turn up the volume again, to see if their score was the same as his. And an amazing percentage of the time he was right. My father said it gave him the spooks. Uncle Rod said it was simply a matter of doing your homework; if you knew the players, you could likely anticipate the outcome. What was hell was pitching changes, he confided. My father told him to cut it out, it still gave him the spooks. Oh, it was worth studying, Uncle Rod said. He bet on the game, too, and let it be known that a person could do handsomely in the modern world, by understanding baseball.

*

The world turned some. Till when when Raymond fell ill we had little time for the sport of finding further reasons to disapprove of Rod. My brother caught us by surprise, because we were distracted by my grandfather, who'd recently gone in the hospital for a prostate operation and was recovering poorly. He'd waited too long for the surgery. (He said a fella oughtna burn his bridges behind him, which disgusted my parents, I couldn't get them to repeat the words, though Uncle Rod took Grandpa's side.) After the operation, my grandfather didn't rebound the way he was supposed to. He lay in his hospital bed with an IV in his arm, a catheter in his urinary tract, which, in delirious moments, he kept trying to pull out. He was lost in the hospital atmosphere, and needed badly to go home. But as his condition worsened, the possibility of going home grew ever more remote.

Then, back at our place, beneath his bedroom walls with pictures of Indy cars whining around corners, for some reason Raymond wouldn't get out of bed. Refused to budge for breakfast. Instead he curled up, one knee pressed against his chest. My parents coaxed and yanked him downstairs and took him to a clinic, where the doctor probed him and was puzzled so shipped him off to the hospital where, after tests and some confusion, during which he was transferred to a motor therapy ward and then back again, they diagnosed a staph infection in Raymond's bloodstream.

Now, normally a staph infection was no big deal—that's what the doctor said—but normally it didn't enter a person's blood. Somehow, though, Raymond had managed just that, the infection had made itself a home there, and at this stage, the doctors said, his problem was serious. My brother lay in a sweat with his mouth open, very still but breathing heavily, as if somewhere inside he was running.

This was my junior year in high school. Raymond was only in the sixth grade, a sparrow-chested boy with brown eyes and bangs trimmed straight across his forehead; he'd never made himself so important before. Our house was upside down. Because first there was Grandpa's situation, which certainly shook us but we got ourselves ready: and then, blindsiding us, Raymond. Getting worse and worse! It's hard to describe how the shock set in. To put it bluntly—we were prepared for Grandpa to die, not Raymond.

But Grandpa hung on, pale and skinny and in stubbly need of a shave. Babbling, while overhead a hospital TV roared game shows. Yet he hung on! While Raymond slipped into critical condition. Our shock wore off, and became tight-lipped fear. There was nothing to do but wait, to see the effect of massive antibiotics.

Then matters grew still more complicated with the question of money. The hospital notified my father that his insurance policy covered only a part of the expenses. (At the lumberyard employees were allowed to buy a special family package from Blue Star.) Would we be able to pay the rest? And how? My father was summoned down to Admissions where they asked him how much money he made. He told them, upon which he was invited into a sunny office on the fourth floor where a man named Mr. Noquay sat beside him on a couch and suggested, in a friendly way, that he consider moving Raymond to another hospital. He told my father that he should be aware of costs and reminded him of his responsibilities, that a fellow ought not put his family in a situation of hardship. There were other facilities that could take care of Raymond. He should think it over.

On his way back to Raymond's room, my father saw Raymond's doctor in the corridor and latched on to him, told him of this conversation. The doctor shook his head: No, no, he was in charge here and it was out of the question to move the boy at present. Maybe later—but for now, we had to minimize risks. No.

That night, however, we had a phone call from Mr. Noquay saying it would be a very smart idea indeed to consider treatment elsewhere and by the way he had contacted both Chicago and Urbana, which had beds available in their facilities.

"But he's not supposed to be moved," my father protested. "The doctor said—"

"Oh, we do it with great care, believe me, it's possible," Noquay said. "There's no need to worry. We make all the arrangements. Your son will even have free ambulance service to the location of your choice. He can leave tomorrow morning."

This conversation went back and forth for ten minutes, my mother hovering beside him, eager to snatch the phone away. My father kept talking louder, turning the phone away. My father kept talking louder, turning his back to her, tangling himself up in the cord. Then he said *"All right, Urbana!"* and slammed down the receiver. He looked at her. His chest heaved, his voice went gravelly. Urbana was further away but sounded surer, he explained, a university hospital, whereas when it came to Chicago . . . . My father's face went slack. He pleaded: "For Lord's sake, Annie, we ain't gonna put Raymond in with a bunch of dopers and crazies and losers."

My parents rode down in the ambulance with him. Raymond was classified as Indigent. My father, who had been at the lumberyard for twenty four years, saw on the papers provided by the first hospital that he was listed as Without Employment. About these insults— and these *were* insults, to him—my father made not a peep for fear this hospital might send my brother away, too. Both my parents moved around in a sort of daze, as if they'd just been clubbed over the head. There were no tears, outbursts—just stunned bewilderment.

In other situations my parents weren't timid, but with doctors and the reception people at Urbana who tried to help them with forms, they acted scared, actually stammering. I remember feeling embarrassed that they were so stupid—I stood back, keeping my coat zipped up and looking at the orange patches of art on the wall, wanting everybody to think I was not with them. How excruciating when they turned around and sought help with a question. You don't even know who you are! I wanted to snap. Isn't it obvious?

Yet in no way were my parents giving up, for they would've signed any paper, told any lie, climbed into that ambulance or if necessary piled Raymond into our Ford with all his tubes in him and driven him them- selves, if that's what it took to get my brother a bed.

Uncle Rod was furious. A few days later he drove me for a return visit to Urbana and on the way he began to cuss. As the mile markers flew by and we passed the trucks, construction crews, an old lady on a moped with visible lettuce in her saddle-bags), he wound himself up into a rage.

"So Ray's indigent, is he?" he said loudly as we entered the hospital room, outdoor air arriving with us. "Is that what's wrong with him?"

Raymond was asleep. My father jerked his head—he and my mother were listening to what a doctor was saying, hanging on to every word. They had no time for distractions. The doctor cleared his throat and continued, saying that Raymond was out of danger now but there was a good chance the bone in his left leg had been affected. Perhaps this leg would no longer grow.

When the doctor left, Uncle Rod resumed: he had no use for doctors, they were miserable bloodsucking gangsters, the lot of them. He went to the window and parted the blinds a crack with his fingers, peeked down to the parking lot, making sure his car wasn't being towed from the Reserved Doctor's Section. "They corner you with their do-goody talk—then collect and collect and collect!" he said. "They protect their turf, Christ Almighty—"

"Shut up, just shut up. This doctor is trying to help Raymond," my father said in a hoarse voice. "He's a good doctor."

But Uncle Rod couldn't shut up, he kept griping till my parents fled the room. They'd been there all night, and looked haggard. "Keep Raymond company," my mother told me on the way out, and I turned to him sleeping there in the bed, his hair sticky on his forehead, not quite believing he wouldn't die.

The room smelled sour. The white walls, white sheets somehow magnified the odor, while the overhead light gave edges a bleached, powdery blue. Uncle Rod conversed with himself about the Doctor Mafia while I thought how I should've been nicer to my brother in the past. And how I should be nicer to him in the future. If he lived. I thought these things, yet I didn't really feel *sorry*; I simply knew them, the way a person answers to her name.

Uncle Rod said doctors should be lined up with their asses to the wall: "I seen what they did to profiteers after the war! There has to be some accounting!" Oh, he had a terrible prejudice against doctors. So I tried to reason with him, if only to distract myself; I said that even if Raymond was an indigent, this room didn't look bad, not much different from the one Grandpa shared back in Seymour. I told him that it didn't seem my brother was getting a bad deal, after all.

Uncle Rod replied that doctors were shitheads.

"But that's no answer," I told him. "You call that an answer? What kind of logic is that? You have to admit that this doctor here's doing good, he's helping Raymond." Uncle Rod shook his head. "What d'you mean?" I said, losing patience. "How can you speak of *all* doctors? They can't *all* be the same, that's just stupid." He shook his head again, and my voice rose higher. "We got the best doctors in the world! We send them everywhere, places where people are ignorant of medicine. You going to say those doctors—like that— they're bad?"

Uncle Rod nodded. "That's right."

Raymond was in the hospital for three weeks. They had to incise his leg along its length and spritz away a deposit on the bone, an intensive, horrible process that preoccupied my mother and father's every thought; they prayed about it each time we sat down at the table. My uncle, since he often passed by at the dinner hour, witnessed these prayers but did not participate; I noticed he kept his eyes wide open during the words. (Mine were open only to check.) The first time I thought he was simply staring at the baked beans, admiring the dark crusty part on top—his favorite. But the second time it happened, he was clearly watching us. When his eyes met mine, instead of winking, as I thought he might, he

84

appeared annoyed. After the Amen he told me across the table: "If you wanna be on speaking terms with God, it's easier if you keep your eyes closed."

My parents frowned but started passing bowls around, grinding the pepper and unpeeling the margarine, unaware of what my uncle was referring to. Rod brought up the subject again after the peach cobbler as he sipped his coffee, while my parents discussed their next visit to the hospital. "The poor kid can't get around it," he put in. "God plays hardball."

My mother shot back before he even had time to lower his cup: "I don't have to listen to that sort of talk." Her eyes were hot. "It's *wrong*. Understand?"

My uncle tried to reassure her.

"Oh, Annie, don't get mad. If you're right then God'll fix me but good. If I'm right—well, the same thing."

A major blow-up was averted only because at that moment the phone jangled, so the discussion of Rod's eternal damnation was put off. There would be plenty of time for that later.

Those days, my parents spent their lives on the road going back and forth to Urbana. My father used his vacation time while at the supermarket I started replacing my mother's shifts. I couldn't go to Urbana because I still had school and someone was needed to stay around for Grandpa. All in all it was a frantic period, though what I remember most was how in the middle of this crisis I sneaked off and had a marvelous time.

One of the fellows at the supermarket had his own apartment, and after an evening shift invited the entire crew. It was so much fun! I danced, more than I ever had in my life, some people were drinking, some people threw up, but I didn't go in for that, I was just dancing to every song. Because there were so many guys who wanted to dance with me. Hardly anyone knew who I was and it didn't even seem to matter—so unlike a school party.

A carry-out guy named Chris kept gliding up to me, shouting pleasant conversation and personal compliments above the music. He had a smooth, happy-sleepy face, his shirt collar turned up, as was the style at the time, and an arresting way of suddenly halting for a second, then dancestepping normally, then halting, then starting again.

"It's called strobing!" he yelled.

"Interesting."

"What?"

"*Interesting!*" I cried.

Then came the slow dances, during which it was easier to converse. After several in each other's arms I allowed him to kiss my jaw but he didn't get my ear. Around us on chairs and even on the floor couples sat on each other's laps and kissed tongue-deeply, fingers pulling at each other's hair.

All of a sudden I pictured Raymond. In his tiled room. Through the throbbing bass and stereo's guitar twangle I remembered the hospital smell. What was my brother doing at this instant? What?

Chris's warm hand was under the back of my shirt stroking and fondling my lower vertebrae—I squirmed, pushed away. He looked at me with a wave of uncertainty moving across his face. For a second I trembled, and almost drew close again.

But I turned, and stepping over people went to look for my coat. Not wanting to cry in front of anybody.

He was waiting for me at the door. "Judy?"

I refused to explain, and pushed past.

It was late by the time I reached my dark, empty house. The first thing I did was flick on all the switches so that the rooms were ablaze. I turned on the TV to break the silence, but the programs stank out tinny and shrill—I snapped it off again. Afterward, the silence seemed more oppressive. The empty chairs and couch looked so beaten, so worn by our bodies.

"No," I said into the silence, and closed my eyes; but now the thought was growing in my head, unstoppable: What if he dies? Is that what God wants? What if he dies?

Now, this fear was stupid, because by then we knew that Raymond was going to pull through; but there was a part of me that for some reason sought out the fear, had an appetite to see it naked. Curling up in a ball I convinced myself in one great swallow, *Raymond is a goner*. Our family would never be the same. We would break up. Such horrible, horrible loneliness!

Then I was running to the kitchen, dialing the telephone, demanding operators, trying to get through to his hospital room in Urbana. (Never mind that the number was taped to the refrigerator door.) Eventually I reached the hospital, and convinced the switchboard that truly oh please believe me it was an emergency. They connected me with Raymond's room. It was 1:30 a.m. There was school for me the next morning. But I had to be sure that my brother was not dead.

An adult voice answered, neither my mother or father—a doctor, I thought, my head pounding. So there *was* something the matter! I knew it! Tears came. "I'm calling about Raymond Gass," I gasped, "I need to know how he is. How is Raymond Gass?"

"Who is this? Judy, that you?"

It was Uncle Rod.

"Uhhh—Yeah. This is Judy."

"What's the matter?"

"Nothing. How's—" Then I blurted: "Raymond's not dead, is he?"

"What?—no. He's the same. The same. The stitches look good. The shitheads say he could be out of here in a week."

"Can I speak to him?"

"He's sleeping now. What the hell is wrong? It's awful late, Judy, is something the matter? Your folks

87

were just talking about you up there by yourself. I said you'd do fine. What is it?"

I was silent, not knowing what to say. I felt a terrible fool. I should've guessed Uncle Rod would be there! Since he had a lot of free time, he was available to go to Urbana.

"Just a sec'," Uncle Rod said. "He's awake now. He can talk to you." The phone scraped. *"Hey Sugar Ray, it's Judy."*

"Judy?" came a familiar voice.

"Raymond!"

"How you doing, Judy? What's goin' on?"

His voice was weaker, there was no doubt about it, but it was definitely my brother. My tears came again, but I no longer felt a fool. I was glad to hear him.

"Listen Raymond, I'm sorry I woke you. You're all right, aren't you? You're better."

He puffed. "Yeah, lots. Me and Uncle Rod are saving water glasses before they throw them away. We got a whole drawer full."

"Raymond, I want you to come home. I want it bad."

There was a pause. "Me too. Me too."

I told him about my new job, gave him the news of his snapping turtle Grover in the basement, and soon I wasn't hating myself. He told me they'd saved a twenty five gauge spinal needle, too. He'd show it to me. When my uncle came back on the line he wanted me to explain, but I said only that I was tired, I'd panicked a little—he wouldn't tell my parents I woke them at 1:30, would he?

"No, not if you don't want me to. But you get some sleep. You hear me?"

That night I lay awake till after four o'clock, my mind racing. Thinking of Raymond. School, work. And many thoughts of Chris. He had no ass. No, just a joint where his legs met his waist. The image stayed in my mind, pleasing. Seemed life would never settle down.

Later, during the table prayer of thanks for Grandpa's having recuperated enough to go back to his place (he complained that we'd moved things around in his absence, though this was false) and for Raymond's having come home, too, I bowed my head with a full heart, sharing in the gratitude. *Death would just have to wait!* After the Amen, as we began to pass the food around, I thought fiercely, *See Rod, what do you know about God? What do you know about hardball?* It was inspiring, we told each other over pork and applesauce. Raymond was going to relearn to walk.

As for me, I was intent on more dancing. My parents thought it was a good idea when I suggested that I continue at the supermarket. Good for my character, they said. After my second paycheck and in time for my next party, I found a pair of tall black suede boots such as I'd always wanted, of which my parents disapproved completely. I was making good money at my job, on top of the extra cash I picked up from Uncle Rod, sewing pockets on tooth fairy pillows.

It was his latest sideline. A pillow with a little pocket on the back, where you could slip in a coin. He thought it was a great gift idea, and paid me fifty cents a pillow. To tell the truth, I didn't believe in the project but did it only for the profit. It was easy. I sewed them faster than he could sell them, and eventually he had to ask me to stop. For a time his glowing room above the cleaners was jammed with pillows, and he said he lived the life of a pasha.

8

Higher Education

By the time I went to college, it seemed clear as rain that my uncle had nothing to teach me. He was a man with no future, lost in his private world, glorious projects headed for bust, the bottom, whatever tight situation he got himself into. He was washed up.

The peculiar thing about this direction in his life was that it was no accident. For most people, losing their future came unexpectedly, as sudden and disagreeable as falling down stairs. My uncle, however, seemed completely aware of where he was going. He'd skipped all the way down with a grin on his puss.

Too bad for him, but the rest of us would keep on doing our duties, planning responsibly and running the world. Back then, encouraged by my parents, I was eager to do my part. "You're on your way to success," my father told me. "Honey, the wheels are greased!" My mother added, "We're proud, very proud, Judy." Happily I believed them and tucked their praises close to my heart.

My first year in college, though, was extremely rocky. The reason wasn't the books, though that's what it looked like when after my first semester I was put on academic probation, an embarrassment to the innermost core of my pride, a wretched secret that I hid from my family by burning the letters from the dean over Christmas vacation when everyone was out of the house shopping. I sneaked around like a thief, leaving not a trace of evidence to betray me.

I'll get through it, I thought. No one's going to take away what's supposed to be mine.

But my second semester was actually worse. By the beginning of April I was failing two classes and slipping badly in a third. I'd thought I would catch up but it just didn't happen. Distractions pulled and hauled at me from all sides. This was the year I learned how to drink, which in those days was a college requirement—if you didn't party and get wobbly you weren't taken seriously—and I went through several boyfriends at the time, which took its toll, though not as much as people think. They were only that, *boy*friends, whereas what I really wanted and was ready for, though I didn't yet conceive of my situation in such terms, was a man. What a joy it would've been to have someone firmly rooted to talk to instead of one of these fellows who thought sincere meant being sulky, or worse, behaving like an excited terrier you had to shake off your leg. That was a good time? Parties were always the same, everybody drinking cup after plastic cup of beer from a keg, and when someone cracked a joke my boy would open his mouth with beer foam in the corners and join the others (whether it was funny or not) in the HAW HAW HAW HAW.

I was lost.

Girlfriends were different, too. Not like high school friends who you just talked, talked, talked to without worrying whether you sounded clever or dumb because it didn't matter, you were friends. Here they watched your every word. My roommate Carrie was very pretty, it was true, and talented—she'd won a drawing scholarship and carried around an oversized portfolio full of her life—but her diet consisted mainly of popcorn (she was trying to lose weight except in her breasts) and her empty stomach made her dreadfully sensitive, inclined to bitch about every detail. "That blind is not how I left it," she said. "Why do you insist on diluting natural light?" And: "Must you brush your hair so loudly?" She relaxed only when her curly-haired boyfriend Marty came over with quaaludes in his hip pocket, which she gobbled with diet cream soda. If she took more than one, the weather inside her changed and her good posture abandoned her, a languor moved across her limbs. Her wrists draped, occasionally a laugh escaped her with a sound like a nail being extracted from a plank. For a time she tried to be more pleasant, sort of flirting with me, till the quaaludes partially paralyzed her tongue and jaw and it became difficult for her to speak without drooling. Then Marty led her by the hand and I would have to leave the room so they could spend some time together in her bottom bunk.

I remember one night when a group of girls from our floor was gathered in our room drinking sloe gin out of dixie cups and telling stories, laughing uproariously, pure silly fun, and when my turn came I repeated a story of Uncle Rod's about a woman from Seymour. As a teenager many years before she'd gotten pregnant, a big shame at the time, so her family kept her at home, wouldn't let her be seen in public. Until, one night, right smack in the middle of the kitchen floor, the baby was stillborn. Her parents took it out to the backyard, buried it beneath the sunflowers.

No one was supposed to know, but the secret got out soon enough. People felt sorry for poor Edith, or Edie as she was called then; she never married but never left town, either. To this day she sang in the choir beside my mother, and no doubt her baby's skeleton was still buried in the yard, beside the house where she still lived, where sunflowers still grew. My mother was flabbergasted the first time my uncle recounted this, and she told him so. My uncle, before he walked out of the room, said (this was the climax, and it was true, too): "Well gee, Annie, I didn't mean to gast your flabbers."

Now, back home, Raymond and I repeated this to

each other, for we thought it was a funny thing. But that night at the dorm, after I finished telling, there was silence. My roommate Carrie, wearing one of her fuzzy cashmere sweaters, arched her back and gave a stretch, smiling a wet, knowing smile. I wasn't the only one to see it—some of the others, too, for an instant had smiles, or traces of smiles.

Then I understood: they thought I was backward. Not one person met my eyes. I froze, unable to breathe another word, then involuntarily looked down at my cup. *The silence.* I'll never forget that silence, its hideousness, my throat tight, the cup in my hand trembling. Finally somebody started another story.

Later, I went to the showers and turned on several full blast, for it was the only place in the whole damn dorm where people couldn't hear you. The water came down and I sobbed, choked, hugging my arms in front of me, unable to stop this sobbing as my whole body lost control, became convulsive. It was hard to stand up, crying so hard, but I didn't dare sit on the tiles in the event someone else should come in to take a shower, and see me.

Whenever I felt like calling home, confessing my failure, announcing that the charade of me in college was over, I thought of my father who spent his days at the lumberyard; I thought of my mother who had never really known a quitting time. For them, the mere fact that I went to college was an end in itself, a success they could claim, a source of relief in their lives. I honestly don't think it occurred to them that there could be such problems *after*: that I would squander their accomplishment.

If Carrie was out of the room (as she usually was during one of my fits of truthfulness) I might slip down to my knees and try to squeeze my will together, force out a desperate prayer. My palms pressing. Oh, to lift this burden upward! But before long I slipped down further and found myself curled up on the floor, seeking distraction from my torment by talking across the tiles into the guinea pig's cage, which Carrie had smuggled into the dorm. I reached out and let the door drop down. "God, help me," I whispered, as the pig looked timidly out the opening. "Please." Then it trotted out happily sniffing, eyes moist and blinking. With a little tempting it would crawl up on my belly where I fed it kernel after kernel of my roommate's unbuttered, unsalted popcorn. Petting provided temporary relief; my eyes watered and it purred gustily, while I repeated, "Hector, just what am I gonna do?"

By early April I'd panicked, couldn't sit still to study, let alone concentrate. One Friday afternoon, facing a chemistry test, the mimeographed sheet with those formulas and those *blanks*: it was more than I could bear.

I knew the score already. Absolutely. I felt like bursting out with exasperation—oh, my chemistry professor's face, so calm, with indifferent, bristly hairs coming out of his nose—I gathered up my calculator and pens into my bag and hurried out of the auditorium, making noise, ducking my head, hoping everyone would think I was sick.

Once outside, I walked for blocks and blocks, my only goal to get away from campus. Put some distance between me and *that*. It was a raw day, a miserly sort of spring, the sun flashing just once in a while through chilly clouds. I had no idea where I was going. After half an hour I became warm and let my coat hang open, sometimes pausing before store windows to stare at a reflection of a girl with messy hair, a big nose, a big mouth: yes, anybody could see, plain as day, a stupid girl.

Eventually I got tired, went into a diner, and sat down at the counter where an occasional wave of trembling ran up my shoulders, pure repulsion. I drank coffee, burning the roof of my mouth, and chewed on a crumbly cinnamon roll that must've been a week old. A newspaper lay on the counter and I picked it up, intending to find an article about a plane crash or something horrible happening to someone so I could feel better. Pain was rising inside me, coming to the surface, refusing to be contained; my breathing was unnaturally loud. As I trembled I began to think of death, how if you lucked into the right one, it might not be so bad after all. There was a student famous on our campus for happening by a boiler the moment it exploded. She disappeared. Absent Emily, they called her . . . .

In a booth behind me, a woman broke out laughing. Her high-pitched voice bounced off walls. My eyes swam; I leaned closer, tried to concentrate on the newspaper in front of me but it was impossible to focus. A fresh wave of trembling, coffee on the paper, then on my sleeve, scalding.

"*Damn!*" I brought my wrist to my mouth.

Another peal of high-pitched laughter. I shot an angry glance toward the booth, where a black woman dipped a spoon in a cup, her head rocking. She didn't even notice me. I looked back down at my reading, the pages shaking in my hands, a soggy stain spreading. It occurred to me as the columns of print jumped before my eyes: *I couldn't even pass a test on this newspaper!* I couldn't! More laughter . . . the woman would not stop. She was splitting my ears! Again, but more deliberately this time, I turned on my stool to give her my coldest, nastiest eye. And this time, she looked up, too. A voice said:

"Well what do you know? Look who's here!"

At the other end of the booth facing the woman sat my Uncle Rod. He looked very small, at that moment, only his red-striped shirt stood out, but then he was on his feet, gliding toward me. "How y'been? Come join us, why don't you?"

I can't remember if I shook my head or not, but he was pulling on my arm; seconds later I was sitting in the booth. Now it was his turn to laugh, with an unlit cigarette dangling from his lower lip. "Good to see ya! You really been hiding yourself."

The black woman, directly across from me, was silent.

She'd seen my stare.

"This is Rosemary," Uncle Rod said. "Rosemary, I want you to meet my niece. She's in college now, really doing something for herself. We're all awful proud of her."

Another wave of trembling, and a terrible sound came out of my throat. A sort of croak. I closed my eyes.

"What is it?" he asked. "Hey—what is it?"

Embarrassed, but feeling so totally lost that it didn't seem to matter what I said, I told him, "I'm sad today. Very sad. That's all."

"Sad?" he said. "Sad?" Uncle Rod paused, and repeated: "Sad?"

I nodded.

"But why?" he asked.

I stared at the table, my coffee-stained sleeve, unable to find the words. I touched my face and felt crumbs there, which I brushed away with the back of my hand. I kept brushing, long after they would've been gone. Once I looked up at Rosemary, who was watching me. At that moment she said,

"You better tell your uncle. He should know. You tell your uncle and he'll help you feel better, that's no lie. He's good at giving comfort. I'm sure he'll understand if you give him a chance to."

Her eyes were not unkind. Uncle Rod took hold of my hand. I felt cornered, at bay in the booth, actually there was no choice—but from the moment I started telling them about my failure, how my future had gone to smash, I felt a relief. Surging. I *had* to talk—the words spilled out. Descriptions of people and sensations that I was convinced they wouldn't understand. Out it poured.

When I finished, Uncle Rod said:

"So that's it. I thought you were pregnant."

He sat back, rubbing his finger on his cheek, visibly relieved. I snapped at him:

"Didn't you hear a single word I said?"

He nodded—oh yes, yes. We stared at our cups for a moment, then he cleared his throat and began to say how it wasn't worth fretting, there'd be a day when I'd see this with a different perspective, a day—

"You're not going to tell Mom and Dad, are you?" I blurted. "Please don't tell."

He looked surprised. Amusement crept in around his eyes, which annoyed me. "Well, no. I suppose that's for you to do. Judy, you're old enough now to do your own telling."

"But I can't. I'll just die, I can't. It'll break their hearts."

He lifted a hand as if he were going to slap the table . . . but he stopped midair. Slid his arm around my shoulder instead.

"Oh hell, quit doing that to yourself," he said. He pulled me closer. "You hear? Really, I hate to see it. Nobody's gonna hang you for this. Times change, Judy. Shit, when I was a kid, Dad would whale on me just because I couldn't tie my shoes and fell down a lot. That's not the way it works anymore. I'm not saying it'll be easy, but you're no kid anymore, not by a long sight—just look at you! Your folks'll respect what you got to do. Take my word."

A calming fatigue came over me. It was less what he said than the sound of his voice, and a sense that I would be able to get through more than the next five minutes.

"They're gonna accept it," he said. "You'd be surprised how much people will accept in the end. Just ask them to accept you."

Why should they? I thought. I don't.

"The man is right," said Rosemary.

Now I looked her in the face. Do you really know this guy? I wanted to ask.

"Sounds to me like you're losing your nerve," he said, jabbing the air. "You gotta keep yourself in the action! I remember back in my ring days how when I had a string of setbacks, I'd take on a few challengers from a Quaker club. I could always beat those guys. That got my confidence built up again, and then I'd be ready for bigger game. That's how I prepared for Harlan the Hammer. You think I was a better fighter than him, when I beat him? I wasn't. He had power, he was one mean clutch puncher. Thought he was so witty, too. I hated that son of a bitch. Listen—I went the distance and beat him because I'd built up my nerve, and I wanted it badder. I danced him into the canvas. Yes, I really wanted it! Maybe that's what you need, too, Judy. You can't stop now. Believe me, there's so much more to be."

I felt my throat burning. "To be?" I said. "To be? What should I *do?*"

"Honey, do what you want to do!" said my uncle, fiercely.

"But I don't know!" I cried, striking the heel of my hand on the table. "*I don't know!* You always pretend everything's so simple, but you can't just do your own thing when other people are counting on you. Rod, it doesn't work that way. People are going to get *hurt.*"

"People," my uncle responded, "should mind their own business."

He flicked open a silver lighter, scratched its wheel with the ball of his thumb, trying to make it flare: stch, stch, stch.

"How can you be so oblivious?" I said. "It's too

easy on yourself, too. People depend on us. People are *weak*. Are you going to tell that to Grandpa, *Do what you want to do?* You know he can't do anything anymore! You gonna say that to suffering? You gonna" (He snapped the lighter shut and looked at me and as soon as he did I floundered, lost myself in a knit of sincerity) "tell that to people who are, I don't know, desperate, hungry? What about—I can just see you going up to some guy crawling out of the rubble after a bomb's dropped on his house, or an earthquake or God knows what, *Hey pal, do what you want to do*—"

"It's the mystery of life, Judy," he interrupted.

"Huh?" I flapped my elbows once, for I'd started sweating.

"The mystery ain't that life's so horrible. Or so beautiful." He leaned back in the booth, his chin rose. "It's that it's so horrible and beautiful at the same time."

He lifted his fists and rubbed his eyes with a screwing motion, very hard, so hard that Rosemary winced. I'd watched him do this before, and wondered if I could trust my memory of a time when I was a child when he'd rubbed them so hard we heard them squeak.

"All you can do," he continued, leaning toward me on his forearms, "is love life as much as you can. Till death do you part."

He hardly seemed the person to cite marriage as a model, but I didn't call him on it.

"Then, Judy, you'll see how you are. Ya follow? In the meantime, maybe I should get in touch with my friend Albert Livingstone. He has a college. Maybe he could straighten this out for you."

I shook my head while across from me Rosemary fingered an antique gold watch pendant. I noticed, showing between the buttons of her blouse, her red bra. Suddenly the truth was so obvious that it seemed pointless to go on. I didn't belong in college—didn't ever want to see that place again. The cookie-cutter hedges and neat brick buildings, the trodden paths through the grass. Oh—a special horror this—those leafy leafy campus trees! At least as much as it was serious, college was an inside joke. Carrie—the others—they'd expected to go, for them it was no big deal. They belonged.

The truth. Clear.

I put my head in my hands, for in my heart I couldn't accept it. He tried to lift me, make me look at them but I pulled away, kept my eyes covered for a long time.

"Judy? Hey, come on. Judy?"

When I finally raised myself up, out of my mouth came the most ridiculous, immature plan imaginable: we could keep it a secret that I'd flunked out and act as if everything was all right, and next year I'd enroll at the Area Tech and if I got really good grades there maybe my college would accept me back the following year, so my parents would never know, and the extra time it took to graduate I could explain by saying I had a quadruple major.

My uncle took a sip of coffee. "Sure, if that's what you want," he said.

And that's what we did. Both Uncle Rod and Rosemary helped me. They found me a cheap place to live after I got kicked out of the dormitory (leaving without saying goodbye to Carrie: that way I could kidnap Hector); Rosemary also found me a part-time job at the hospital to pay my bills. Not a bedpan job, either: kitchen work, decent, clean. Rosemary was a nurse, had been to college and knew what it was like. In the '60s her brother Cannie had played seven years as a switch-hitting utility man in the major leagues, another very positive feature about Rosemary, as far as Uncle Rod was concerned.

When news eventually circulated in the family about the new woman my uncle was going round with, it created a stir. My grandfather, who confused most things nowadays, grasped this situation instantly. "Let's just hope they don't go too far, have a zebra!" When my father said he thought it was getting a bit late for that, Grandpa sneered in his face. My father accepted the news with a sort of resignation, and didn't seem too bothered, as long as he didn't have to talk about it. This had become his attitude about many things, such as my brother's leg and the biennial appointments so the doctors could break it, put in steel-bolt extenders. As long as you didn't *talk* about Raymond's appointments, my father didn't act upset, unlike my mother, who a month before a bonebreaking session suffered from stomach cramps and diarrhea, had trouble sleeping, and went on crying jags. When she wasn't working at the supermarket with horrible dark circles under her eyes, she shuffled around the house in her bathrobe in the most irritating way. We begged her, please, to change.

Raymond was a good-looking kid, not stupid in school, too silent, maybe—but to mention his appointments was like a slur on him, my father would not abide it; while my mother positively *ached* to talk about Raymond's leg, to be reassured that really, it was everyday business. But how could you say that?

So it was with a hungry sort of fury that she fell upon a subject like Uncle Rod's love life, which cost her no pain, about which, she KNEW. Her voice rose, sardonic:

"You see how low he's sunk. I think he gets a sort of pleasure out of it. He likes to see how low he can go. That's how I understand him."

Aunt Pat, who'd recently dyed her hair peach, shared the same opinion. She came around our house less than before but was as ever up-to-date, especially on a subject like this. "Can you believe it?" she said. "In *our* family." Her eyes grew wider. "A man of his caliber!" Her twins were finishing their studies at the State University, and the university was sorry to see them go, from the way Aunt Pat told it. The place wouldn't be the same afterward.

She and my mother had no idea how well I knew Rosemary. How I'd met her sons. (Rosemary was divorced, but I didn't volunteer this information.) Above all, how helpful Rosemary had been to me. At times I wanted to throw all this in their faces. Douse them with some truth.

But that would mean confiding my secret. So I let them rave on, and when I got to feeling too guilty, picked on them about other things: if they made a grammar mistake, I went out of my way to point it out and correct them, which they accepted humbly, feeling stupid, for after all, I went to college.

9

Dandelions

Grandpa died on his kitchen floor. He caught us by surprise, for he'd seemed to be doing better only a few days earlier when my father took him for his monthly visit to the eye doctor. (Ever since his return from the hospital he'd had endless problems with his glasses: they no longer stayed on his head. They kept falling off. My parents got him new glasses, tried several sizes and styles, but nothing worked—they refused to stay on. Once I witnessed it myself—they jumped off his face.) The last time my father took him back to his house he persuaded him to use an elastic band, though my grandfather had protested it was too tight on his brain.

Several days later, my father found Grandpa dead on the floor. He spoke of it in a hushed voice, how kitchen chairs were tipped over, how my grandfather had one shoe on, one shoe off, and a ripped sack of oranges in front of him—oranges had rolled everywhere. What was particularly disconcerting was the path my father found, a trail of disorder leading all the way back to the bathroom. Evidently he was trying to crawl to the telephone.

"But he hadn't lost his Goddamn glasses. The band held, just like I'd told him. But—he deserved better than to die that way. I just can't stop picturing him, what Dad—why does it have to finish like that?"

"He wanted to die at home," my mother said.

"Not like that!" he retorted. "What're you talking about?"

My father acted offended, though she was only trying to comfort him and he knew it. In a peculiar fashion
he *needed* someone to say something objectionable, so
he could bark. His eyes glowed before she even opened
her mouth. Then he repeated what he'd seen, the
upended chairs, the explosion of oranges, the glasses
strapped tight—his face clouding in pained incompre-
hension.

This time my father insisted on taking care of the
funeral arrangements, a hopeless task, for Grandpa had
let it be known beforehand that no matter what we did,
he wouldn't be satisfied. The problem had been brew-
ing for years, going back to the day Rod bungled
Grandma's burial. An unfortunate misunderstanding,
but for my grandfather a question of principle.

What had happened was this: a few weeks after
Grandma's funeral and the furor about Uncle Rod's
leather pants had subsided, Grandpa noticed that
Grandma had been buried on the left, whereas according
to him, she belonged on the right. The two plots were
reversed.

Everyone tried to tell him that it didn't make any difference, right or left. Why worry about such a thing?
But Grandpa fretted, and insisted, "Jennie always slept
on my right, it's a fact and there's nothing or nobody can
change it. She belongs on my right."

He'd always been a very neat man. Uncle Rod felt
bad about his error, and before leaving for Florida, tried
to console him. He told Grandpa it depended on how
you looked at it. If you stood at the other end, she *was*
on his right. Grandpa let out a hissing breath, shook his
head violently. "You don't look at it that way, any fool
knows that. Stop talking like an idiot. It's the stone, the
stone that decides."

"Well, in that case, we can turn the stone around."

Grandpa flushed, his fingers twitching uncontrol-
lably. "Don't you humor me now! Turn the stone

around! Turn the stone around?" He would discuss it no further. The mere idea stressed him: every other stone facing the other way. Why, he'd be the laughingstock of the cemetery.

So when he died, my father considered digging Grandma up, giving Grandpa her place, while Rod thought we should start all over with a new set of plots, because after these two were used up, what about the rest of us? He said he could swing a special deal where he worked. He had connections.

But there was a hitch: the new plots would have to be at a different cemetery. Transport of Grandma after fourteen years underground would need to be arranged. This required lots of paperwork, notarized statements and forms in triplicate, and in the end my father and Rod got so frustrated at trying to unravel the death code in the brief interval before the funeral that they changed nothing. Grandpa finished up on Grandma's right.

"It's not like I didn't try," my father apologized, to the air.

"She came *first* this time," my mother said with satisfaction.

Rod, his eyes rimmed red, told them: "It comes to the same anyway, no matter where we put him. You're out of reach down there, it don't change. There's nothing to do but suck the roots of dandelions."

In the funeral pew that day I cried. My grandfather had been in many ways a spiteful man, a wrongheaded man, a man who hurt people who loved him and worst of all never forgave, never—yet I cried to see him go down. The bad things receded. Death had a way of flattering people.

*

Grandpa's house got an astonishingly good price despite its crackerbox size and the repair it needed.

Afterward, to our dismay, the buyer didn't fix it up but brought in a bulldozer. A convenience store sprouted on the space. There were gas pumps where my grandfather used to plant his winter onions, a fish bait machine in his kitchen. A pair of video games hulked in the phantom of his front door. Such developments created a stir in Seymour. It was the first place in town to be open all night; before, you had to go down the road six miles.

The sudden influx of money came in handy for my parents, for breaking Raymond's leg and putting a new roof on their house. At least in this respect the timing couldn't've been better. Uncle Rod spent his share of the sale proceeds on a new apartment, moving out of his room above the dry cleaners and into a smart little duplex with a tinted skylight at the Maugham Estates. He bought a new low-slung Japanese car, too. His inheritance, however, served only to underscore a fact we'd begun to notice over the last few years: Uncle Rod had money (as my father put it) out the ying-yang.

We became aware of this slowly, though there were plenty of signs before Grandpa's death. He launched no new schemes yet at the same time mangaged to live more comfortably, ate restaurant catfish three times a week and smoked Dutch cigarettes. During my college days he occasionally slipped me sums which would not be obvious for a part-time night janitor at the Van Allen School of Mortuary Science. Where did he get this cash? It would've been rude to ask and besides, Uncle Rod wasn't the sort of person you questioned too much. Experience had taught me not to.

But it was unmistakable: over a few years my uncle's standard of living had soared. His new apartment boasted a pearl suede couch, brass sink fixtures, a black bathtub with claw feet. In his bedroom an enormous bed—a triple, I think. His clothes, too, changed. Not overnight, and not as conspicuously as where he lived, but he cultivated a more refined appearance—

108

even if, in his way, Uncle Rod had always been a snappy dresser. His canary tie of shimmering silk was a permanent fixture in everyone's memory, we'd seen it at holiday meals for twenty years. But now there were other silken beauties ("Worms can be the *busiest* little fellas, eh? eh?"), magenta and India black and robin's egg blue. And his amazing, blazing Japanese rising sun! You had to avert your eyes. When you could corner Rod into going to church (say, for Aunt Pat's twins' double wedding), on these occasions he wore the softest grey pinstripe suit, a tie the color of deepest burgundy gravy and blue-black shoes that possessed not so much a shine as a mysterious, mineral-like gleam. No one in the church looked so dignified. Senator Gass, my father called him.

But where did the money come from? What accounted for this turnabout at his age, when men like my father seemed resigned, letting themselves go physically, marking time till retirement—yet also more nervous, jittery, emotionally frayed. The worst of both worlds. My father's blood pressure situation got so bad that sometimes when he grew excited vessels in his nose would burst and he would have to thrust his handkerchief to his face to catch the blood. Sometimes, if my uncle noticed my father getting agitated, he would warn his brother to calm down, watch out for those fragile blood vessels: Uncle Rod touched his own nose, chiding, "Pop pop, Carlton. Pop pop."

For my mother, aging carried an added ingredient of self-abasement. Once, after Raymond had remarked that her greying head looked like a dustball under his bed, she sought out the same beautician as Aunt Pat for a deluxe dye job. Her hair came out purply plum, at which point my brother told her: "Gee Mom, now your color matches the circles under your eyes."

She began to cry. She turned around and tromped upstairs to the bathroom sink where she plunged her head under a faucet and tried to wash out the dye. (In vain.) She sputtered at the mirror and plunged again, for a remark from Raymond hurt worse than one from my father. He was the ace. I marveled at his cruelty, and also at how she could care so much about the opinion of a jeering son who held out hoops for her to jump through, and each time she tried, he pulled away.

So it was a merciless age, the toughest transition my parents had ever been through. Even Albert Livingstone wrote to say that he was a recovering alcoholic. My uncle's contrasting health and youthful appearance were rarely brought up in my family—they struck too close to home, maybe suggested a queerer sort of Providence— rather, comment tended to center on his material ease, a curious thing in a man who'd never been known to run after money. (Or even, according to my mother, to break into a trot.) We knew that my uncle's inheritance from Grandpa wasn't enough to set him up for life. Sometimes my father wondered aloud if his brother had devised The Perfect System for wagering on baseball, and was now raking in the benefits. The Van Allen School of Mortuary Science was only a cover. He asked my uncle point-blank if this was true, and Rod grinned.

"We all place our bets in this world," he said, spinning his forefinger in the air. "Round and round she goes, where it all stops or where you drops—nobody knows!"

Of course my father must've felt a little jealous, after the meager fruits of faithful years at the lumberyard, to see his brother doing so much better. How did he pay for his diamond-studded tie clip?

"Jeez, those ain't real rocks, are they?" my father asked.

The clip glistened, caught and refracted the light. It was the one touch of ostentation my uncle allowed himself with his senator's suit. The effect was perfect: Uncle Rod smiled, his eyes becoming crinkly. He looked down at the quiet splendor of his shirtfront.

"Ya like them babies?"

When I graduated from college (on schedule with the Six Year Plan), he and Rosemary were the first persons I wanted to thank. By then, though, they had gone their separate ways. When I tried to find out why, my uncle hinted that Rosemary's family had appreciated him even less than our family did Rosemary. Pressure had been brought to bear. "You know families are like that," he said. He shrugged several times, then straightened his cuffs. "Goddamn picky. What can I say?"

He let on that it was no big deal, but as he spoke a puckering around his mouth gave him away. My question still stung.

Maybe it was the aftermath of Rosemary letting him down that explained these changes in his appearance. There was the inescapable fact that if he still wanted to be a good-looking man, he now had to make an effort. Dressing the dude was just another way of fighting back Time. And he invited the rest of us to join in the campaign to sparkle: one Christmas he gave everyone flashy jewelry.

We opened the tidy boxes, gaping at the contents, then let the springy lids snap shut as we looked up for instruction. *What?* We couldn't begin to guess how much these mounted gem beauties had cost, since we never bought such things for ourselves. By then I had a steady job of my own in telemarketing (like my uncle, I showed a knack for salespersonship)—but I spent my money on a down payment on an apartment, on repaying student loans, on a health plan. Not cluster brooches!

"What does Raymond need an ID bracelet for?" my father asked us as after Christmas dinner when we'd moved into the living room and he paced in front of the TV, looking at his watch and talking to us till his show came on. (The disruption in regular programming caused by the holiday put him in a bad mood.) In the kitchen, a second pot of coffee dripped. He frowned.

111

"And *gold*, for God's sake, who knows how many karats. It's the most pointless thing in the world!"

"Well, it is pretty original," I ventured, thrusting a shoulder forward and lowering my chin, trying to peek at the light in my brooch.

My father turned on his heel and inhaled, pulled up on his belt, gathering what he could of the front of his pants. Then he let his stomach out again. "But what's the point? Annie, the kid knows his name already."

My mother answered with a cough then shook her head at my father's belly, perhaps thinking of the quantity of turkey and potatoes and cranberry sauce inside, which was truly sickening. "But don't you know?" she replied eventually. "The bracelet doesn't even say his name. It says Andrew."

"Andrew?"

My father rubbed his jaw and pondered. This was Raymond's middle name, which he'd never used before. It was also my grandfather's name. At that moment my brother came back from the bathroom, flopped on the couch. He looked over at us, and froze.

"What is it? Stop looking at me! What is it? Why's everybody looking at me?"

"We were just talking about your identity," I told him.

He relaxed, with his lips made a bluttering sound. He shook his arm, and the ID bracelet flashed into view.

"I don't like that kind of thing," my mother said.

Raymond shrugged, for he didn't care. My mother was suspicious of jewelry on men.

"Annie, leave 'im be," my father grumbled. "It's a present!"

Now that he saw a link with my grandfather's name, no one could speak ill of it.

Raymond brought the bracelet closer to his face, scratched his fingernail over the engraved letters, and shivered.

112

I told him, "Gee, you must like the fact that you can be someone else. I don't blame you."

"What's that supposed to mean?" my mother asked. "Why are you always so unpleasant?"

"Yeah, what is that crap?" my father said.

Raymond saved me, jackknifing off the couch and limping away. "Andrew—who cares? It could be any-body."

10

My Uncle's Confession

As a wedding gift, Rod gave my husband Gary some gold sea-horse cufflinks with emerald eyes. Gary thanked him very much, then at home confessed to me his perplexity about what to do with them. "My shirts aren't like that. I've never used cufflinks. It's not that I don't appreciate the thought . . ."

He put them with a *chunk* on the table. It was awkward initiating someone new to the family to Rod's excessive generosity and unreasonableness. I looked at the sea horses, so out of their element here, washed up under the lamp of our kitchen table God-knows-why, and admitted that my uncle could've chosen better.

"He meant well," I said. (Hoping it was true.)

"Oh I know that. Of course he did. Maybe you could use them? You think you could have them transformed into earrings?"

As soon as I picked them up, it was obvious that they were too heavy. I rubbed my earlobes. "No, I think they would hurt."

He considered for a moment, a finger stroking a cheek. "Doorknobs?" he said. "Jesus, Judy, what are we going to do with all this gold?"

It was true that our needs were more practical. One could hardly imagine Gary wearing such cufflinks while he deboned a chicken or steamed his angel-hair pasta or chopped twenty gallons of lettuce. In Seymour's old downtown square stood a brick-front building, originally the fire station, that he'd bought and remodeled into a restaurant. He did much of the work himself, lowering the ceiling and putting in new tile; a contractor replaced the huge fire-engine exit doors with a ledge of matching brick and frosted windows, so at night the place emanated a pleasing golden glow. At the time of our wedding Gary was in the process of negotiating with my uncle on a walk-in refrigerator system, top of the line, bought at cost from the Van Allen's supplier. "This, sweetie, is something people can use," he said.

Gary had grown up in the restaurant business; his family ran a steak and spaghetti house in Utah, where he'd been raised a Mormon. He was a direct descendant of an original founder of Deseret, and had been expected to continue in the church. Instead he'd dropped out of college in Provo and before doing his missionary service, left his home state and made his way east to try a different life. He'd lived in a number of cities before coming to the Chicago area, worked in a care facility for retarded adults, sold orange juice concentrate at trade conventions, even done farm labor in Norway, before deciding to go back into what he knew best. He'd chosen Seymour to invest in because it was less saturated for restaurants than the city, costs were lower. He rarely returned to Utah though at the time I met him, Latter-Day Saints still occasionally knocked on his door. His family had contacted the locals in the hope of bringing him back into the fold.

My family thought they were lively good company and tolerant to the point of being magnanimous but that did not spare me mortifying moments. My father seemed to think that being friendly with Gary consisted in asking questions about the Great Salt Lake. He did this repeatedly, inquiring about its shape, its size, its fishless briny depths. How about swimming there? Was it true that it was virtually impossible to drown in that salty water, you just bobbed like a cork? Fat people scarcely got wet? I tried to distract my father but he grilled Gary on the Great Salt Lake every time he saw him. Gary had to go to the library to look up information in order to have something to say.

My mother's reaction was worse. She took me aside one Saturday afternoon "just for a little talk" and, pulling at my hands, wanted me to reassure her that Gary wasn't going to haul me back West where maybe in the shadow of some dry new Canaan mountain he already had a wife and a bevy of indoctrinated children who responded to their father's every word with robotic obedience. Oh yes, she said, that sort of thing still happened—she'd read so in a magazine! Judy, her only daughter—with a bigamist! Maybe a trigamist!

. "You see me in a harem?" I put in, and she gazed at me, her eyes growing wider.

"You are ignorant, just ignorant!" I told her, jerking my hands away. "Keep your advice to yourself. You hear me?"

"Judy—"

"Just shut up!"

She paled . . . stared at me up and down. "Never in my life would I have spoken to my mother that way," she whispered. "Never. Judy, do you know what you've done?" Then she left the room, refusing to cry in front of me.

I stood in the middle of the rug. Now the house seemed empty (no longer my house anyway) so I went out and sat in my car. Looked at the sky and pin oak tree, then pressed my forehead against the steering wheel, sick with myself for my meanness.

When I gathered my composure, I looked up at the house again. It was time to go in and apologize. She was waiting. I reached out, turned the key, and drove away.

The most troubling reaction to Gary came from my Uncle Rod, for in his case the insult occurred in his presence. It happened on the weekend before the wedding when my uncle had invited us for cocktails up in his new apartment. He had concocted a sweet froth in his shiny shaker, we were sipping, laughing, enjoying ourselves, me in a favorite burnt orange dress and Gary wearing black jeans and a vaguely sailorish tight white shirt (in which it must be said he looked very fine), when suddenly my uncle spoiled things by shooting off his mouth about religion.

"Something I've been meaning to ask you," he announced as music flowed and sprinkled from his imported German speakers, and one foot of his crossed legs tapped the air. "Do Mormons go in for Jesus?"

The question popped out so oddly, unattached to anything, that I winced. Why was he bringing this up? Gary reached in front of him for a handful of cashews, and thumbed one between his lips. "Why, yes. They do."

"Hmphh," my uncle said, leaning back on the couch cushions. "*Puh.*"

Gary stopped chewing, picked up his glass and took a quick sip. I looked back and forth between them, not knowing who to stop first. I wanted to tell Gary as he eyed the man: Wait a second! Don't misunderstand! (In private, Gary sometimes let fly sharp remarks about his people back home but a comment from someone else was different, a comment from someone else had to be fair, precise, spot on exacto: the skin just above Gary's mouth drew tighter, tighter, as if he could smell bigotry.) "That's enough," I told my uncle.

What Gary didn't realize was that Rod had nothing against Mormons in particular; he was prejudiced about Jesus in general. It was all very unfair—maybe something to do with his chocolate memories, but whatever the reason, it wasn't anything Gary should take personally. That was just the way my uncle believed. Sometimes, to hear him speak, you would've thought Jesus was a doctor, not a carpenter.

118

"Enough?" he said. "Hey, I got plenty more."

He rose to his feet and started mixing a second batch of cocktails. Bottles glugged and spissed, he added ice, screwed on the top and threw his whole body into short, convulsive motions. Shake shake shake. Shake shake shake. Disconcerting to watch, like a man with his finger caught in an electrical socket. Then he stopped, panting a little, and unscrewed the top. He reached over and sloshed more pink mix into Gary's glass—"Have some more, man," then, laughing, turned to me. "Judy?"

Already I was flushed, my kneecaps tingled. These drinks were strong. I shook my head, and he poured me another anyway.

"Be sociable," he said.

Ever since he'd got this new cocktail shaker with fancy carrying case (coded lock and crushed velvet interior, like for a musical instrument), he'd pushed such concoctions on people, running in and out of the new apartment's gleaming, NASA-like kitchen for long-stem coupes and grasshopper glasses. My last memory of my grandfather before seeing him lowered into the ground on my grandmother's right, was of Rod forcing a cocktail into his spotted, trembling hand, and of my grandfather staring down at the glass, its swizzle stick and green parasol, saying he'd never sipped a cocktail in all his eighty five years and *he'd be goddamned if he was about to start now!* He wouldn't even look up as he spoke, but stared at the drink in his hand, his face darkening with outrage, distress, and great bitterness.

Rod lifted his glass. "Let's have this one for Jesus. No offense of course, *henc henc.*"

Gary watched him, unsmiling.

"Uncle, *please,*" I said.

"Everybody always wants me to excuse myself," Rod said, grinning at Gary.

"I'm not asking you to excuse yourself," Gary told him. He downed his glass in a gulp. "Why are you telling me that?"

"Jesus was sinless. I don't know if I trust that."

My lips felt numb and I pinched them, for an instant my vision shimmied. Gary pivoted toward him and waved his glass, squinting, pointing a finger. "What's the matter with being sinless?"

"Trust a guy who never did anything wrong? Think about it!"

Then he was refilling Gary's glass, then his, while I pulled mine out of reach. Rod was just getting started, his ears and backs of his hands coloring pink. "Don't pull a long face, Judy, I want you to understand. Jesus goes *wayyy* back. Let me tell you. No, let me tell you! You know they sent me and your dad to church back when we were kids, week after week, and I'll come right to the point: once I was doing something I wasn't supposed to do, embarrassing—all right, I was picking my nose, okay?—and my Sunday school teacher told me to stop it. Now hear me out! I never did like this teacher. She was always snipping, and here I was picking my nose just a little, on the side, discreetly, bothering no one. Still she jumps right on me about it, like it was a mean thing to do. Well, that day the lesson was about the boy Jesus in the synagogue, answering all the elders—I remember the lesson, because it had a lot to do with what happened next. I assumed Jesus would understand what a pain in the ass my teacher was. I straightened up, asked her if she thought the boy Jesus ever picked his nose. Her eyes got big. She couldn't believe it! I thought she was going to slap me. Certainly not! she says. Jesus never picked his nose. I was a spiteful, nasty boy to say such a thing.

"And from that moment on I became a doubter. I mean—who never did it? Even *once*? I'm sorry—but that's how it was, when I was a kid, I can't help it, and in all honesty I've never been the same since. I guess I could pretend and tell you something that sounded finer, more sophisticated, but it was that day when I was a kid that opened my eyes. How could this Jesus be for real? How can you take the guy seriously?"

"I refuse to get into it with you," I told him. "You're completely beside the point!"

"Must be, must be. Up there on the cross, just think of it, even if his nose itched he was out of luck, I'm not saying he didn't suffer. But—hey, just kidding there, oh never mind, Judy, I'll stop. Don't make those sadful eyes, you take me too serious. Religion's never been one of my good subjects. Some people are like that, you know. Religion just doesn't stick. It ain't that I want to roast in hell like a pig on a spit. It's like, like when some people can't sing on key. You see? So I can't help it, I'm sorry. But you know I *can* sing on key—actually I enjoy some of those hymns, they got punch. *A Mi-ighty Fortress i-is our God,"* he began, *"a bulwark never fai-ai-ai-ling."*

Gary stared. Oh, I wished we could leave now! But I couldn't get his attention, he watched my uncle, his head tilting further and further to one side, his hands gripping his knees, then there was a strange instant when his head lolled suddenly like a dashboard dog's but he righted himself so quickly, not batting an eye, that a moment later I wasn't sure it had happened. While Rod talked and talked, ever the host: should he shake me and my fella up another drinky?

*

"You think it would be all right to sell them, Judy? I had them appraised and you wouldn't believe how much gold is there, how much they're worth. You know, I could live without them."

I looked at the plump sea horses on the table.

"Sell them?"

I was caught short. Even if the cufflinks had been a foolish gift, cashing them in wouldn't have occurred to

121

me. I had hoped that, despite clumsy beginnings, in time a friendship would develop between Gary and my uncle. After all, the refrigeration deal had come through for the restaurant. Now was Gary acting out of resentment, or just being practical?

"These'll pay for the new plumbing and central air and insurance for a year, honey," he explained. "They're worth that much! But I won't sell them if you're against it."

After a few days mulling it over, I consented. Though it would've seemed more in the spirit of Rod's gift to use it to defray an extravagance, a trip to Mexico, say, the sea horses weren't intended for me, and if Gary had other ideas, who was I to object?

"Listen," I told my husband, "don't worry about trying to understand the man. You'll see how he really is."

11

Hard Currency

A minister later observed that the Lord's ways were especially mysterious when it came to Uncle Rod. Maybe that would've been the best manner to react in when the news hit, when the police started prying. I don't understand the public's attraction to morbid details.

A bereaved son had stopped by unexpectedly one night at the Van Allen School of Mortuary Science to see his dead mother. The school offered special rates to the public, the best prices around, for the students provided the labor. (My grandparents' funerals would've passed through the Van Allen if my parents hadn't felt too queasy about it, though Uncle Rod insisted their standards were as high as anywhere else—and they had the clientele to prove it.) The son had stepped into the sitting room reserved for vigils, which was darkened. When he flicked on the light, he caught my uncle in the act.

Uncle Rod stood at the coffin, bending over his mother. Hands around her neck.

The son screamed. Uncle Rod looked up, startled. The son got a good view of his face before Rod scurried out a side door. The son still screamed, backing out of the room. A student-intern who was on duty that night, a big tight end on the Van Allen football team, came running from the front office. The son described what he'd seen and though the student-intern was skeptical (only a week before a coffinside visitor had claimed to have sighted a glittering angel), together they searched the premises, passing from room to room, looking under tables and behind doors. They found no one. Everything was in order. Just as they were about to abandon their search, the student-intern opened a supply closet. There stood Uncle Rod among his brooms and buckets. Again the son screamed. Uncle Rod said nothing, but reached forward his hand, dangling a necklace.

He made the newspapers again. Not for the first couple of days—our family didn't even know he was under arrest for the first couple of days—but later, when the charges against him and the scale of the operation became public. He wasn't the only one in on the scheme. A Chicago jeweler named Burke was the main party. (This must be made clear: the blame hasn't yet been fairly apportioned.) Uncle Rod got a lot of attention in the papers and on the six- and ten o'clock news broadcasts. But Burke was the big organizer, had been for years.

Uncle Rod confessed everything to me, and told me of Burke's primary role, the first day I visited him at the jail. They hadn't set a trial date yet, for they were still looking into the possibility of further charges. My uncle was poorly shaven and looked very tired, with more lines on his forehead than ever before. His clothes were disheveled. They'd taken away his robin's egg blue tie, in the event he might hang himself. He still managed a smile though, when he saw me. "Hey, Judy. I knew it!"

Trying to sound natural but failing completely in these circumstances (I'd never been to a jail before, and what I saw was like the bad cousin of the hospital— lightbulbs unshaded, and instead of the odor of ammonia there was a damp smell of yeasty molds and a taint of piss), my voice quavered: "Knew what, Rod?"

"Knew you'd come. You're my true blue."

Through the wire mesh of the visitors' chamber he described the whole sordid business. In the beginning, when Uncle Rod was on his own, he stole very little. Only once in a while. And no one missed what he took, for there was a list in the top drawer of the assistant director's desk of every item on the body of the deceased, every piece of jewelry, and which pieces were to be returned to the family after the service, which were to be buried. Uncle Rod had a passkey to the office, and could consult the list whenever he felt like it. He took only items that were to be buried, from people with closed-casket funerals. Mainly wedding rings, little trinkets. For years, no one missed them.

"Don't think it was nasty, something dirty-sneaky underground," he said. "It was more like a little bird eatin' cherries at the top of the tree that no one's gonna reach anyway."

In his efforts to sell his pickings, he came to know a number of people in the jewelry business. It was Burke who urged my uncle to cultivate a larger supply, and who, upon learning the source, suggested using items that would be returned to the family, too. All Uncle Rod had to do was borrow them for a short time, and Burke could replace stones, then Uncle Rod could return the new model. It was foolproof—the family didn't know the difference, so they didn't feel cheated. They could go on for years or even generations happy as ever with their beautiful heirlooms. And if somewhere down the line they found out their real nature—even if they took them to be appraised and sold immediately after the funeral—well, they simply believed that Grandma had led them on a bit, perhaps innocently; one mustn't judge too harshly the departed . . . .

"The little bird turned out to be, well, a slyboots. *Henc henc.*"

I was the first to learn the complete truth. When my uncle telephoned from jail after the story hit the newspapers and TV stations flashed his face on the screen, my parents were too shocked to listen to him. Uncle

Rod told me how my father kept interrupting, "*Oh Lord Jesus, I can't believe you went this far, Rod, can't believe you went this far,*" not giving my uncle the chance to explain what precisely he had done. "*For God's sake, man, you're not well.*" Then my mother grabbed the phone and screeched at him: "*What about my ruby ring? What about my ruby ring?*" Since he'd given it to her long ago, she hoped it wasn't from the Van Allen. But Uncle Rod, to his credit, was truthful. Did she remember old Mrs. Carter, the one with liver cancer and bird binoculars who always put out the flag? Well, he'd gotten the ring from her—

My mother dropped the phone. Raymond and my father still talk about that night, how my mother pulled and pulled on the ring, but couldn't get it off. Unlike Raymond's ID bracelet, which he'd managed to lose after only a week, this piece of jewelry seemed attached to its new possessor. My mother tried soap, and butter, and paraffin—followed by big greasy smears of Vaseline—but to no avail. My father was afraid he'd hurt her, when she wedged her hand between the back rungs of a chair and begged, in tears now, for him to pull harder. He told her, "Annie, your finger could break! It could come right off," and she sobbed, "If it does it's all his fault!" Eventually my father couldn't stand the tension any longer and, fearing for the blood vessels in his nose, went out in the backyard and stood in the dark for a while. He said he got madder than he'd ever felt in his entire life at Uncle Rod, that somehow everything just built up inside him, all the memories, and he started stamping on the ground where the dinosaur hole had been, nose or no nose, and beating his fists on his thighs, under the moonlight.

Then he stopped, for he realized he didn't trust my mother.

He hurried back into the house, in his panic imagining her with a steak knife.

He found her in the bathroom telling Raymond to hurry as he pried at the ring with a pair of pliers. "We've gotta get a grip on ourselves!" my father shouted at them, "we just gotta!" Raymond and my mother looked up. Raymond said afterward that my father wouldn't stop yelling these words, my mother was sure his nose would go off any second, they couldn't calm him, though my father denies this part.

Eventually all three of them made it out to the garage where my father took his wire shears but since his hands were trembling so badly had to give them up to Raymond. (My mother has a steadier hand than either of them, but he didn't trust her.) Raymond snipped the ring off.

The county jail was the worst possible place for Uncle Rod. If the community wanted to punish him, it certainly succeeded. The dampness of his cell gave him blinding sinus pain. He truly suffered. This discomfort might last for hours; it was a frightening thing to witness. On more than one occasion under the cell's bare bulb I saw my uncle close his eyes, grit his teeth at the pain; in moments of desperation he extended a fist in front of him, then jerked it back quickly, giving himself a left jab.

His bail had been put at an outrageous sum, utterly out of keeping with the offense of theft, because he was also charged with violating a rarely invoked clause in the state code, which forbade defiling the dead. This crime, according to the book, was of comparable seriousness to child molestation and rape, so Uncle Rod's cell was in the section of the jail reserved for the Highly Dangerous.

I tried desperately to raise the bail but there were obstacles at every turn. It was an exasperating experience; until you have a loved one in jail (everyone *should*, at least once, I came to believe afterward), it is impossible to understand the sense of helplessness. The outright repulsion of others for your every appeal. The most hurtful blow came from my parents. Just when Uncle Rod needed them most, in a situation that asked us to forget our differences and rally round—it could've been our family's finest hour!—my parents threw up their hands. Uncle Rod would have to take the consequences of his actions, they said.

The timing was bad for money matters since Gary and I had sunk almost everything we had into The Firehouse (we'd let the name stand for the restaurant because that was how many people in town still referred to the location, and that way everyone would be sure to know where to find us). I'd quit my old job to manage the front office, handle reception and receipts, while Gary was in charge of all the ordering and food preparation. Our cash flow, I was well-placed to say, was at that time a mere dribble, so to raise my uncle's bail we'd need help from the outside. Putting on a dark navy skirt and silk blouse and matching pumps, with a cherry scarf for color (my job-interview ensemble), I went to the bank.

Despite a carefully rehearsed speech and my better-than-average credit rating, the bank officer, a Mr. Randall, refused me. This was an outrage, as far as I was concerned, for had I wanted to buy a fancy car or redecorate the apartment, or take a vacation in the Virgin Islands, he would've said Yes. But when I told him I intended to get a family member out of jail, he said No, they weren't that kind of institution. "Well what kind of institution are you?" I asked, standing up, feeling color rise to my face. Mr. Randall merely smiled behind his desk, very respectable.

Afterward I tried another bank and pretended it was to put a new charcoal pit in the restaurant, but they wanted to know why Gary and I weren't borrowing from our previous lender. And did he entrust such requests to his *wife*? "Frankly, you haven't proved yet that you're a winner," they said.

And after that, a grimy little bonding company wasn't even interested in the mortgage on the apartment. "You've barely started paying it off," said a round-faced man with a terrible cold who was preparing to eat a sandwich on his desk. He didn't even turn off the radio when I entered the office, and while I made my pitch he poked in pieces of shredded lettuce that had fallen from between the pumpernickel slices, breathing heavily, as if the task might be too much for him. "You want that much money?" he asked, lifting his head, his eyes watering. He snuffled long and deep, then swallowed. "Nope. Might've been possible a few years back but right now, real estate's too slow in this town."

A wistful look came to his face, he leaned closer—was he having second thoughts?—then I jumped. Under his desk a hand had started to climb up my leg.

"You're very attractive, I want you to know that," he said.

Back on the sidewalk, walking fast as these shoes allowed, as if launched from a slingshot. Dusk was falling. "Damn it, we are not helpless!" I exclaimed. "We are not!" Eventually I slowed down, dragging my hand along a storefront, each step on the concrete moving up my body. My Uncle Rod behind bars. With my other hand I pressed my fingers against my temple, now praying, "Oh please free him. Something's got to work." It was like an unhappy music seething in me. *"Goddamn, we are not helpless,"* and *"Please free him!" "Goddamn!" "Please."*

What we needed was a coherent plan, a strategy for our next move and the one after that, but after these efforts to beg money my brain was sliding backward. No, I didn't have enough for bail and didn't even know where I could try next. It was as simple as that. All I owned were memories, and these were too numerous and sometimes not very good, no reason to be sentimental. Recollections came to me in stabs and snippets right there on the street. My uncle's attic room, the smoke

129

trailing out of his rattly old Polara. Beth shouting at him that he was a liar. The tightness around his mouth when he walked out of the room on his way to Florida. His leather pants.

That was the problem, my head was too full of these things. They were personal possessions that I was incapable of putting away, that I carried with me everywhere and looked at while around me echoed the sound of other voices. Whether good or bad, these things had been. And as long as I carried them, in a certain manner they would still be.

"Goddamn . . . Please!"

Now came the image, hurtling up from some far corner of my mind: the dinosaur's kneecap. It stopped me on the sidewalk, before my eyes a dirty yellow, its texture rough and smooth at the same time: giving itself to the touch. Bone. Bone. As if I could reach into my purse and pull out—*this. This,* oh you judges, was the currency I carried.

12

Visitors

My parents wouldn't even visit my uncle, at first. Gary and I were the only ones to go see him. We went in the morning, Gary excusing himself after a few minutes to take care of the day's shopping for The Firehouse. Once, though it was against the rules, Gary brought along a rack rib dinner and all the trimmings for my uncle, and after tense negotiations with guards an exception was made on the condition that none of the food went beyond the visitors' area. Rod had to consume everything immediately. That morning I did all the talking while my uncle dug in, shoveling, sawing, and chewing. Occasionally when I said something he agreed with, he nodded while sucking a bone.

Rod appreciated this gesture from Gary very much. On my next visit, when we were alone, he told me, "I used to wonder what you saw in that guy. I used to say to myself—at least she didn't marry a doctor. But that was hasty. He don't say much but he knows what he's doing. Not just his barbecue sauce—that's not really so hard. The man makes serious coleslaw. You can tell him I said so."

As for the rest of the family, it was only after I described to them how much Uncle Rod was struggling, and diminishing, that my father came. It was a fact—each time I saw my uncle, he seemed smaller. In jail he was like a plant that had been put in the dark. He was getting yellow around the eyes. Aside from his one-day feast on a rack of Gary's ribs, the food in jail was a major problem for him, his regime of canned macaroni and instant potatoes depressed him terribly. He told me of waking up in the middle of the night after a vivid dream of being a boy again and devouring a squirrel in sour cream and lemon. There was no question of satisfying such appetites here.

When my father finally visited, the change in his brother's appearance affected him profoundly. All the recriminations he'd reminded me of in the car were cast aside.

"You—you look tired, Rod."

"Well, that I am. In this place you get worn out doing nothing."

"Are they . . ." my father searched for his words, "are they extra rough in there?"

"Oh, that depends what you mean. We got heat, they feed us their baby food. This is nothing like I saw during the war, Christ, I'd never claim that. But I'm not as young as I used to be, Carl. I'd got into my habits."

"I mean, I hope it's not dangerous."

"Like, are they buttfucking me? Naw."

My father appeared greatly relieved. He announced that he'd brought my uncle a radio.

"I want you to feel at home," he said. "That is—oh you know what I mean."

"Yeah, thanks," Uncle Rod said. He called a guard over to inspect and approve the radio so it could be brought around to the other side of the mesh. In a few minutes Rod was fingering the dials. "We got TV here during the day but those shows're hard on a person, 'specially the ones that are supposed to be funny. I don't go in the TV room anymore."

"So what do you do?" my father asked.

"Oh—we talk, sometimes. They let us smoke as much as we want. A fellow has plenty of time to think, like last night I got this idea how a person could make a bundle." His mouth twitched a little at the sides, and I could see he was preparing to tease his brother. "You

132

could invest with me, Carl, after I get out of here. The idea is this: heart-shaped toilet seats. You see? Natural! Whadya—"

My father waved his hands in front of him, his face pained. "Oh, no! P-please . . ."

Rod laughed. "Just kidding, big guy, I was just kidding!" Now he smacked his fist on his palm, his face broke with pleasure. "In jail I figure there ought to be a reprieve for my jokes. Boy, I really had ya going. You'll believe anything."

My father didn't join in the laughter. He swallowed, replied, "You don't leave me much choice. What can I do but believe?"

Uncle Rod still grinned. "That's what I like about you, brother, you know that. Only next time let me reach a punch line—"

"Listen, Rod—"

"Actually, business and toilet seats couldn't be further from my mind. What I find myself thinking about in this place is you people. A lot." He paused, smiling at me, too. Already he looked better than when we'd arrived. His eyes shone. He lifted his gaze beyond my father and me, though obviously no one was there. "Where's Annie?"

My father shifted his weight. "Oh—you might as well know. She's still pretty sore."

Uncle Rod put the radio under his arm, pushing in the antenna.

"Yeah. I figured that."

He cleared his throat, waiting, but my father didn't elaborate. After all, my mother was still inclined to punctuate her opinions about Rod with violent gestures, her hands slashing the air. According to Raymond, her flabbers were gasted beyond repair. (Though when I listened to her abuse my uncle, a different image came to my mind, an image so clear that it should've been obvious years ago: a picture of them together, in the ring.)

Now I wished Rod would apologize. At least admit

he was sorry for the consternation he'd caused. I'm sure that's what my father was hoping, too. But the silence stretched on, on, uncomfortable, till eventually Rod asked me,

"How's your little brother?"

"He's, oh . . ." I fumbled for a moment, before lying: "Raymond says hi."

Uncle Rod gave a grunt, pleased. "Well you tell him I wanna see him. He should come for a visit. He still ripping around on that motorcycle?"

"Oh, don't even say it!" my father exclaimed, his nostrils flaring. "He got another speeding ticket right in the middle of downtown, sixty five miles an hour! I'd like to pound some sense into that kid."

Uncle Rod let out a whistle. "Carlton, I've tried to talk to him."

Raymond had graduated from high school the previous spring but still lived at home, working in the Country Mall as a travel agent trainee. He'd bought an extremely fast motorcyle on credit, a bright yellow Yamaha 750 Crotchrocket (with an electric start—he couldn't kick), on which he tore all over town, roared through residential blocks, screamed down highways. My parents hated this motorcycle, everything about it, hated it with unyielding passion. My mother had exploding yellow nightmares about it; my father said he'd never be able to keep up the payments, he was squandering good money on a fool's toy. Even Uncle Rod had come out against the machine. Shortly before he went to jail, he took Raymond aside and told him a story of a fellow he'd known in his youth who'd seen action at Guadalcanal and managed to come back to America in one piece, only to kill himself on a motorcycle in our hometown, *"Cut his head off,"* Rod insisted. *"Cop had to pick it up, carry it over to the meat wagon."*

Of course Raymond was unaffected upon hearing this, unless he became surlier. He raced around even faster, took the 750 out on country blacktops when there were piled green clouds and tornado sightings. Once he missed a corner and plowed into a cornfield—by the time he stopped he was in so deep he didn't know how to get out. Lost in the stalks for hours. When I tried to speak to him about changing his behavior he grew foul-mouthed, which was supposed to intimidate me; when my mother implored him to stop using bad language, he replied in a high sweet voice, "Okay then, you old poopy." She turned away, grieving. All in all he conducted himself in a very silly way, and refused to help around the house or participate in expenses, spending his money only on his 750, his traffic tickets, and his kid girlfriend barely out of junior high whose pants were so tight she was visibly sliced—Ginny—who followed him around with a snaky walk and wore patches on her jacket and was always licking her large, very chapped lips. She and my brother got drunk together on Blue Nun wine before lunch: my parents didn't know the half of it. He was the sort of I'm-so-tough skulking boy I would've detested but for the fact I knew it was only Raymond.

"You tell Ray I *asked* to see him," Uncle Rod said. "I wanna talk to him."

"Yeah, I'll let him know."

At that point I left the brothers together and hurried to a drugstore near the jail to buy some batteries for the radio, because the guard had confiscated the plug-in cord in the event my uncle might want to electrocute himself. When I returned and had the batteries passed through, I suggested to Uncle Rod, stupidly, "Now you're all set. I bet you can find a ball game."

With patience, yet with a tiredness sweeping across his face, he answered, "Honey, don't you know that the season's over?"

As we spoke, a clicking of heels sounded on the concrete floor, at first far away but getting closer, louder, louder, till we turned and saw, escorted by a man in uniform: Rosemary Woods.

When she discovered my father and me standing

there, my father hitching up his pants as he does at least sixty times a day and me staring and clutching an empty drugstore sack to my breast, Rosemary smiled. "Yes, these *are* the people!" Her voice rang clear against the cinder block walls. Although I was very glad to see her, in my surprise I didn't know what to say. Somehow I felt my father and I looked lame, very inappropriate, at such a solemn moment.

At the sound of her voice Uncle Rod, who couldn't see down the corridor, said in a hoarse, incredulous whisper, "*Rosemary?*"

"How're you doing?" she said as she came beside us. Her red coat hung open, she wore a white uniform underneath. She must've come straight from work. We should've hugged or something, but we'd never touched before and we didn't now, either. She stopped smiling and pursed her lips, shook hands with my father, then edged past us, to the holding cell. She seemed plumper, with a snowy skiff on top of her hair, which she now wore very short. Otherwise, she appeared the same. She beamed.

"Hey, Big Rod. Hey."

"Hey Spearmint."

There were tears in his eyes. He was breathing hard, his mouth twisted.

"You look terrible," she said. "Uck, Big Rod. What's going on with you, anyway? What're you doing here? My sister Dolores saw your face on the TV. Why did you have to go and get your face on the TV?"

"PLEASE—no touching the prisoners!" said a voice behind us. We all jumped, having forgotten the presence of the guard. His voice wasn't mean, but it was unnervingly flat and empty. Rosemary and Uncle Rod jerked their hands back from the wire mesh.

"Thanks for coming," Uncle Rod said. "Oh Rosie, I can smell the fresh air on you."

"Breathe, Big Rod," she said. "Breathe."

13

A Tremendous One

Our lawyer said our best hope lay in pursuing the jeweler Burke. We had to get him to assume his share of the blame. He was, after all, the major player in this affair, in charge of most phases of the operation. Why should my uncle be the only one to pay a price?

But Burke was cagey. Though he was under investigation, the police hadn't pressed any charges yet. He wasn't about to hand over evidence against himself the way Rod had. With each day fresh reports came on television of families protesting they'd lost precious stones and metals at the Van Allen. Some of their stories were surely false or exaggerated, but at that stage no one cared about substantiating the claims.

"*How* can they lie so brazenly?" I exclaimed to Gary one morning in the Firehouse kitchen. I'd just listened to a news segment on the car radio on the way to work, full of wild allegations, and upon arriving had stomped through the kitchen's swinging doors. "To hear some of these people, you'd think they were relatives of King Tut!"

Gary stopped chopping, swept chunks of a bell pepper onto a plate that he sent sliding down the counter toward his next work station. He observed, his knife moving in the air, "There are those who'll stab you in the back—" a flick of his wrist, "and there are those who'll stab in the front." Now he flashed upward. "It feels worse when you see it coming."

And there was no getting out of the way! My uncle was painted as a ruthless grave robber; our good family name was vilified. Not one newspaper showed mercy. The lowest blow came from the Chicago *Counselor*, which announced: "Missing Organs Linked to Grisly Gass."

In fact my uncle was no longer recognizable in what was said about him. Some people were excited with the money side of the scandal, imagining him richer than he was, more powerful. Others thought of him as gross or degenerate; evil, even. And still others had it in their heads that surely beyond the crime Rod was present to make a statement, symbolic of something. A meaning had to depend on him. But in truth all this was only, as my father blurted in the living room as he tossed printed sheets on either side of his easy chair, "horseshit!" Although in our family we might not have Rod completely figured out, we knew him well enough to see that for many he had no identity but what was projected on him. The fact that the papers had run a picture of him with a jacket over his head when he was arraigned at the courthouse only made things worse; people's imaginations were tingled.

Why couldn't all these people accept that Rod wasn't going to fit some stupid script as small as their minds? With such lawyer talk, always in the name of something different they constructed a realm of fallacy. A prison of words. Enough! I wanted to cry. The truth, however strange or simple or unknown, deserved at least a measure of respect.

But truth was not in fashion. Everywhere you looked there was the same shabby weave of lies. Whenever I or Rod's lawyer tried to speak to Burke, we were immediately rebuffed, and obliged to deal with his lawyer, a Mr. Theodore, who gave the impression that Burke had never heard of Uncle Rod (who??), much less touched his jewelry. Mr. Theodore treated the affair as an unfortunate misunderstanding, and presented himself as sympathetic to my uncle's plight. Oh, he would like to help me, but alas, that was impossible. "If my client can assist you or your uncle, he surely will! I can relay a message to my client, if you wish. I'm here to be of service."

Uncle Rod's appointed lawyer, Sally Barnes, reassured us that a plea bargain was inevitable. The defiling charges might be dropped, even grand larceny, if we could show that Uncle Rod had acted merely as an accomplice. It was just a matter of time, she declared, and waiting for the necessary formalities. We mustn't act too pressed because in the event Burke were charged, we would gain leverage.

"Sit tight," was her philosophy, "and eventually you'll blend in with the rest of the scenery—many an accused fades away before the prosecution's very eyes!"

"I am sittin' tight," Rod told her dryly, exhaling smoke, smashing a cigarette on the sole of his shoe. While meeting to discuss our indictment strategy, she'd asked that he not smoke. So he gazed back unblinking, a sour look gathering on his face. "They got my ass in stir. What else *can* I do but sit tight?"

"Think: mistrial!" she said.

Sally Barnes was young and smart, and liked to talk snotty to police guards, the District Attorney, just about everyone except Uncle Rod and me. With us she was peppy. My uncle certainly could've done worse, I realized, when I saw the other court-appointed attorneys around the jail, fat-bottomed men with coffee stains, briefcases, bags of jelly donuts. Yet somehow, up against Mr. Theodore and his gold-rimmed glasses and smooth manners, I felt we were at a disadvantage.

Uncle Rod had erred—I told him so myself, as a matter of principle: he'd screwed up badly this time. Yet in my heart I could not judge him absolutely. It hurt me that he'd done wrong, and truly disturbed me that many worse wrongs, cruelties, had been done and were still being done by people using the excuses of Rod (I saw this plainly and when it came to cruelties, would not yield an inch). Still, a terrible struggle broke out in my heart for my uncle the individual. How could I refuse him? There's the bad he's done, I thought, and there's the good he is. A principle's a fine thing, you can admire it all you want, but an individual's more complicated. An individual, you love.

How could I separate myself from him? I didn't want to. In the beginning I even tried to convince myself that if my uncle were a thief, he must not be an ordinary thief. He was not a defiler—at least no ordinary defiler!

Yet he refused to reassure either Rosemary or me, his most regular visitors. "Sure I stole," he said one day, sniffing. (Not with remorse but because of his sinuses.) "And they caught me, and now I'm up shit creek. That's all there is. Don't preach, or look too far, Judy. The reason I'm sorry is that I got caught. That's what I regret—being stuck here in the Cop Shop. If I hadn't got caught I'd still be stealing, okay? I'm giving it to you straight."

"But you know stealing is wrong," I replied. "Straight words can lie, too."

"Oh, child! I'm not sure you even want to understand. Do you think that if everybody were just *nice* and *kind* to one another, everything'd be all right? Smoooothed out, like? Well, it's not so simple. You gotta look at the guys in here with me, these people. Some of them might be better, with kindness, some—but I'm telling you honey, that's not gonna fix most of them. We got people in here who are like downed electric wires after a storm, if you could see them, just twitchin' around. They'll hurt you! And you can't undo the storm, or pretend it never happened. You might think your ideas can change the weather in the future—though I'm not holding my breath on that one, either—but that'll do nothing for these guys. They've been through the storm! Or it's still going on inside. And it's no joke, they *will* hurt you!"

I scooted my chair closer.

"I'm not talking about them," I said. "I'm talking about you. And me. You're not answering me."

He puffed his lips, for this annoyed him.

"What—what? What do you want to know?"

"What do you think? *Why* you did it! *Why* you put yourself in this place."

He broke into a slow, easy smile.

"Oh. Is that all? Come on now, Judy—how can a person put a finger on a reason why, when nothing's ever so specific as that? A person makes a way in life, and sometimes stealing comes along as part of the package deal. I started making my way a long time ago, girl. It's true your father wouldn't've got himself into a fix like this. He made himself a different way. And far be it from me to criticize your father. He's a good man. Your mother is a good woman—"

"Don't change the subject on me now!"

His face grew stony. "I'm not. Maybe I can't tell you exactly why I'm here, but Judy, I have a pretty fair idea of when, in my head, I started making certain choices. Your father was important then, he was there. You ever hear what his first job was when he got back from the war? He never talks about it, but he didn't start off at the lumberyard. That's a lie. Did you know that?"

"No," I said.

"I didn't think so. When Carlton got discharged from the service his first job was at the grain elevator. Dad helped him get it. They gave him a shovel. And he said, All right, what do I shovel? Your father had a build on him, he didn't fool around. He thought he was going to empty a truck or something.

"But they told him to kill the rats. *That's* what the shovel was for. So your father went out back where they pointed him and started doing it. Blang blang! I'm not making this up. If you didn't kill them the first blow, they'd come after you, they'd attack, Carlton told me.

You had to be fast. He did that for weeks! That's the difference between your father and me. I wouldn't kill the rats."

He paused, then suddenly brought a fist down through the air, first to the left, next to the right, swishing in front of him, crushing phantom attackers. And just as suddenly, he stopped.

"A little later your father got on at the lumberyard, and Dad kept pushing me to take the rat job, but I refused every time. Don't get me wrong—I'm not knocking your father—but it's true. I set my mind. Your father knows it. Actually I'm sorry that he *hides* that he killed the rats, instead of talking about it. It's an ugly thing but for the guy that's doing it, it's something— everybody else just wants to hand the shovel. But I never wanted to do that neither. Not in this short life. You follow me?"

I nodded, but wasn't going to let him dwell on the past. He could be so slippery.

"It's not like you were some Robin Hood," I told him. "Maybe then we could give your stealing the benefit of the doubt, but when you take stuff from other people just for yourself—unless you're hungry or something but you weren't, Rod, not you—how do you expect anybody to accept your reasons? Rats or no rats, Uncle Rod. That's not even an *excuse*. Come on, wasn't it wrong?"

"Oh, not always just for myself," he said, tapping around his sinuses with his thumb, "there was you, too, a little, and Raymond to help pay off the gangsters. There's the Los Hijos Little League Development, and now they got that Triple-A ballplayers bone marrow fundraiser. Not everybody gets dished out the same amount of luck, anybody can see that. And that's what Miss Barnes wants me to talk about in court. Tell it like I was some Robin Hood."

This made me pause. At the mention of the money

I'd accepted from him over the years, a wave of uneasiness ebbed in my stomach. I thought, too, of the brooch in a rosewood box at home, of the gold cufflinks Gary had sold. (Ever since Rod's arrest we'd been apprehensive he'd mention the sea horses with emerald eyes in one of his statements to the authorities, which would put Gary and me in a fix, for we couldn't get them back. Eventually we might be able to pay for them, yes, we could try to raise the money. But pay whom?) Still, at the same time, I felt a wild hope in my heart upon hearing Sally Barnes' plan for Rod's defense. Maybe it was true, maybe it would offer the explanation, the cure to our problems! Then my uncle's actions would make sense, and anybody could understand his reasons—the judge, the jury, the newspapers, people in town—everyone.

"But that's bullshit. Like you say, Judy, I wasn't some Robin Hood, and the more I think about it the more I doubt I'll go along with Miss Barnes. Mostly I stole for myself, not for others, there's no getting around it, and not out of hunger but 'cause I felt like it, it was easier than working more and sometimes, just for the sheer pleasure. If I'd been in it for others I could've done a hell of a lot more. A hell of a lot. Others—they were the exceptions. It was for me, the tie clip, not because I needed to pay the rent but because it was a beauty. Never seen anything like it. Wasn't going to let Burke get his hands on it, no way. And this toothpick—" he reached into his pocket, extracted a pick in its gold holder and began to poke his gums, chuckling—"this little dandy is the one thing they haven't took away from me. They're not going to, either. I ever show this to you up close? The initials—"

"About a hundred times."

"Oh. And by the way, I need some replacement picks. Next time you come around you think you could smuggle some in?"

He was serious, yet all the same I felt he was goading me, too, the way he goaded my parents. "Why do you talk like that?" I asked. "To *me*, Uncle Rod."

"Just tellin' the truth. You don't want me to sin, and it's a sin to lie, just like it is to steal. Funny how if I start telling the truth, I'll be asking for a lot more trouble. That's what it really boils down to. Miss Barnes doesn't want me to tell the truth, anybody can see. Maybe *you* don't either, Judy. You wanna hear it? The truth is, when I stole, I let the dead people watch me. All right? It became like a rule with me—they watched."

"Watched?"

"That's right. Started from almost the very beginning. Once, there was an old lady whose earrings I was taking and it happened she had her eyes open, and, well, it bothered me. I got all nervous and shaking and couldn't hardly stand it, those eyes—and then I *couldn't* stand it, so I reached over and closed them. It felt strange, but it was easy. I'd seen the barber at Van Allen do it. Really it's nothing. Just a touch. But after I done it, I felt so mean. Taking from a dead person and not even looking her in the eye! Now that's mean! So after fretting around for a while I reached over and opened her eyes, and believe me, that's a lot harder. You got to work at them, squeegeelike. But I done it, and felt better for it, and took the earrings. She was dead, she didn't care."

"You—you scare me when you talk like that."

"Oh hell, child, so many people walking round are just as dead and they don't even know it. You think they love how they're living? I seen them with my own eyes, every day. To tell the truth, I doubt there's much difference between taking from most people who're up and about, who don't profit from their breathing, and taking from their relatives who don't breathe anymore. Only difference is, taking from someone who's stretched out on the slab is easier. That's all. They don't get all huffy.

And that's why I chose them. I'm not a guy who likes to put up with static."

"But you've hurt people!" I exclaimed—was it possible even to discuss with him? "Don't you see that your actions have other consequences?"

Uncle Rod took a deep breath, looking at me through the wire. He nodded.

"Yeah," he began slowly, "yeah, I've hurt people in my day. Sometimes it couldn't be helped, and in those cases there's nothing to say. Nothing. You hear me? Other times, well—it could've been helped and so, then, I'm sorry. Truly I am."

With both hands, he pressed on the bridge of his nose, so hard the muscles in his wrists bulged. Then he gave a little sniff. He went on,

"But this ain't neither of those cases, Judy. These folks I took from had cold bodies, which wasn't their fault—but none of these bodies is complaining, are they? I never heard one. It's all these others, the relatives who're still breathing and people who watch newspapers and believe what they say about me on TV, these people who get so stirred up and upset. It's the still-breathing, the warm bodies, who're the troublemakers, with the cold hearts. Maybe it's them I defile. I defile their deadness. I consider myself a success at that. Maybe I ain't so respectable. But I'm alive, Goddamnit."

He paused, ran his fingernail across the wire mesh, clicking.

"Uncle," I said softly, "Uncle, you make me think of some advice you gave me once, once when I was in a bad way. I've never forgotten. Maybe I haven't always been able to believe it, but I still think about it. You spoke about being how you want to be. About loving life. Now I'm going to ask you, since you made the choices that put you *here*—" (I ran my finger on the mesh, too). "Are you how you want to be? Are you loving your life?"

Maybe those were mean questions. I've thought back on them, sometimes with regret. But he didn't miss a beat.

"I'm working on that. Not saying I've gone the whole nine innings but I'm working on that, Judy. People don't appreciate how much I am, how much I've always been, a working man. You believe me, don't you?"

My finger went through the wire, tried to touch him. "Yes, I do."

He winced. I was taken aback, but then he jammed the heel of his hand to his nose, roughly, a number of times in quick succession. So I understood it was his sinuses. When he lowered his hand his eyes opened wider, he moved to the edge of his chair, and his chest expanded. A faraway look, total abandonment, flickered across his face.

When the sneeze came, it was tremendous. His body snapped like a whip. Then he came to rest, suddenly, looking at me through the mesh with a curious, surprised expression, as if greeting me for the first time. The color drained from his face. He inhaled deeply, then slumped back, fell off the side of his chair.

"Uncle Rod! Uncle Rod!"

When a guard came forward he hesitated, as if it might be a trick.

"Open it!" I shouted. "Open it!"

The guard refused to budge until another guard arrived a few moments later, and even then I wasn't allowed on the other side. The first stayed with me while the other entered, turned Uncle Rod over. He put his hand to his chest; and then, cupped it in front of his nose.

He looked back at us.

"I'm afraid he's dead," he said.

14

Grief

Yes, Uncle Rod died of a sneeze. Or more precisely extreme sinus congestion. Or even more precisely, as the doctor ruled, of a brain aneurism, no doubt resulting from the tremendous force of his eruption. Death or at the very least paralysis was inescapable in cases of such morbid dilation.

Many people present that day at the jail heard the sneeze, though I was the only one to witness it. Later, there was a merciless barrage of questions from authorities about what had happened, literally hours of interrogations. These were uniformly petty, with little regard for a person's feelings.

I argued against an autopsy, knowing how appalled Uncle Rod would be by the idea of doctors cutting open his heart, sawing open his head just for curiosity's sake. It would confirm his suspicions, which I'd spent so much energy denying. But my father had the final say as he was legally the closest kin, and he went along with the authorities who insisted that an autopsy was necessary. Before long I understood that some investigators suspected Uncle Rod of suicide, and me of being an accomplice—a ridiculous theory, for never would I have helped my uncle kill himself. Nor would Uncle Rod have planned such a thing in the first place, a preposterous idea for one who so readily courted life. Only once in my recollection I'd heard him mention suicide, how he'd considered it back in his younger, wilder days, but like so many things at the time it had seemed too much of a commitment. As it turned out the autopsy vindicated me by proving the obvious: my uncle had acted involuntarily.

Grief is a strange emotion. The first day I hardly felt a thing beyond a shaky excitement, irritation at my questioners, and outright disbelief. The image of my uncle on the floor replayed itself over and over in my mind. There was no sense. As if what had happened remained somehow tentative, and hadn't entered the truth yet.

The second day the loss was overwhelming and I cried. Cried with the cut-open soul of a child. Refusing.

Never, I remember telling myself, never—even after time had passed and the number of events behind me numbed my outward manners and this pain in my chest could be called a memory—never would I put aside my anger at this loved one's unworthy end. This was my choice, yet also seemed to come from my uncle himself . . . Was this how he'd felt when he was alive? Though to others I regained composure, acted as before, a passage had rerouted inside me. Death sang in my head, and whistled like air in my bones.

I certainly hadn't asked for it. The last gift from a thief. Give it up? No, *never*.

For the rest of the family, too, the shock was great. Though they couldn't share in my sentiment, nonetheless they were appalled by the circumstances, caught off guard by such a sudden demise. My uncle had survived childhood, adolescence, a World War, imprisonment, and a .35 caliber bullet; countless jobs and failed careers and the grief of broken relationships; the death of his parents; and ultimately scandal and universal ignominy—only to be felled by *expurtus coxictorum*, so the coroner's report said.

The Van Allen School wanted nothing to do with Uncle Rod's body, but a couple of students who'd been fond of him and were still loyal despite the bad press saw to it that he got a fine pine box with red cedar struts, a special limited edition from the Classics series, which they told me had been one of my uncle's favorites. A small local funeral home handled the rest.

Looking at him in his coffin as he lay in state, I was struck by a transformation. At first I couldn't place what it was, though clearly it had something to do with the jut of his cheekbones and the swerve of his hair, the way it was pulled back. Actually, Uncle Rod looked younger. Disturbingly so. There was nothing pleasant or reassuring about it.

Suddenly I recognized the expression on his face from an old photograph. Yes, that was it! Not the Army photo, which I'd confiscated after Rod's death, and now prized—but the one in his high school yearbook. The same bewilderment, in the eyes.

I turned away, walked to the back of the room at the funeral home, the two rows of empty chairs. There should be more people visiting, I thought. There should *at least* be more flowers. The prisoners on his jail block had sent a wreath, which I appreciated, but where were the other recognitions that ought to have accompanied Rod's—anyone's—passing from life?

I sank into a plush red cushioned chair. The carpet here was similar, even the walls. This funeral home was a ghastly place, no doubt about it, yet somehow I didn't know how to react, for I was all cried out. It occurred to me that the visitation area was like the interior of my uncle's cocktail kit, and I smiled to myself.

Raymond stood nearby—tall, sullen, pained. Before coming here today he'd had an argument with my parents about what clothes he should wear. The funeral service wasn't until tomorrow, so he saw no reason to get dressed up. He didn't see what the big hairy deal was . . . .

My parents drew near the coffin. My father breathed heavily, talked softly. "You were all right, Rod. You didn't have to go like that. You didn't."

149

"Poor Rod," my mother said, bringing her gloved hands together, pressing her small fists, looking down, "poor Rod." Even at this distance I saw she was crying, and hoped there was forgiveness in her heart. "Peace," she said, "Peace."

15

The Last Request

Rosemary came to the funeral service with one of her sons, I think it was Lewis, a tall young man with a neatly trimmed goatee, striding seriously down the aisle, keeping his eyes straight ahead. (How he'd changed in a few years!) She must've brought him along for moral support. Rosemary was visibly distraught, her chin close to her chest, and even more conspicuously apart with her son beside her. They could've sat next to me but I was already between Gary and my parents. She kept her distance, but during the hymns I heard her voice rising.

Throughout the service I listened to the minister's prayers about Uncle Rod's soul, feeling very troubled. My uncle's *soul*. On the one hand it seemed an appealing idea. A spring of hope. Yet if there were really going to be a reckoning, if what people said was true, he hadn't been repentant enough of his wrongdoing, of this I was sure.

Still, I found myself clinging to the notion that an Almighty, if such a Rash Being existed, would make some allowance for my uncle. Give him a break, I thought. If no allowance was forthcoming, then I felt very disappointed in God. What about an uncandied Jesus? I knew Rod would laugh if he heard such thoughts (Maybe, I wondered wildly, Uncle Rod did! He could hear my thoughts!)—and Rod's indifferent laughter, which echoed in my mind, troubled me even more.

"*Henc henc henc.*"

With a cold tightening in my stomach I thought of

my own death and the possibility that Rod was right, the possibility of nothing, nothing but a dark hole of eternity. Perhaps the last experience I'd have in common with Uncle Rod. My heart was filled with anguish, a longing, reaching for something else.

At the graveyard the minister started into his routine immediately for it was cold, and the wind bit. His ears were pink, his dark tie flapped over his shoulder and stuck there. In the distance parked under a tree stood a yellow digging machine, big teeth ready to cut the frozen earth. A man in a red down jacket and cap with open earflaps tinkered at its side, preparing to dig someone else's hole.

The minister began talking about mysterious ways. I found it hard to listen, rubbing my arms, hoping the minister would see me, thinking, Hurry. Hurry.

"Let us pray."

At least my uncle would have a fine gravestone, I told myself, breathing in a draft of cold air, picturing the speckled granite tablet buffed to a mirror finish that I'd picked out (my parents had left this decision up to me; the stone would be ready next week). In the cemetery, of all places, my uncle would get the respect which was his due. In the cemetery he would be treated as well as all the others.

Then, as I was thinking this, something shocking happened. That is the only word. There was the closing benediction, after which my father threw a handful of dirt on top of the coffin, and my mother and I threw flowers, some of which the wind blew out of the hole and around people's legs and beyond, where they scattered among other stones. Raymond took a turn, then limped away as fast as he could. Behind him was Rosemary. When Rosemary approached the grave, she spat.

Everyone saw it. She didn't spit ostentatiously, as if trying to insult us. But it was unmistakable, a fleck of sputum leaving her mouth, caught by the wind and shooting with remarkable velocity into the hole, disappearing into the dirt.

"Wha—" my father said, stunned, unable to finish even one word. He repeated himself, "Wha—?" Distress now shaking every limb. Suddenly red streamed, collected on his upper lip.

I was no better. Gasping, speechless. The minister's hands dropped to his sides, he threw out his chin, staring.

My mother was the only one who managed to react. She came to Uncle Rod's defense, exclaiming, "*Who do you think you are?*" In her hand she held a last flower, a broken iris. She threw the flower at Rosemary. It hit her in the chest and fell to the ground. Tears rolled down Rosemary's cheeks.

Lewis tugged at her arm, his eyes wide, horrified. He tried to pull her away but she was a big woman, and would not be moved. "*Big Rod asked me to do it,*" Rosemary said, her lips trembling. "*Long ago. He asked me.*"

Final Word

So I've got the chocolate Jesus molds, the baseball books which don't mean a thing to me. Gary picked up one but said it was too dry. The books are filled with newspaper clippings that crumble to the touch. Up against the staggering sum of a person's life, words are the shortest of breaths, a book is a last-ditch witness. Aunt Pat tried to get her hands on the Army photo (some people have gall!) but that was out of the question. It was the one souvenir I had to have. For the rest, there is not much else that can be done. An unanswered Christmas card from Albert Livingstone lies in our kitchen drawer.

Actually, Uncle Rod left this world with very few material possessions. The diamond tie clip was restored to the family of the original owner, and the strings of wedding bands found in a shoebox under his bed were auctioned off, the proceeds going to those who'd filed claims against the Van Allen. Rod's gold toothpick, to the best of my knowledge, was last seen in the possession of his defender Sally Barnes.

I must mention, though, a particular packet of letters that came into my parents' possession, and which attracted my interest. To tell the truth, I went through all of Uncle Rod's old love letters, under the pretext of trying to find the necessary information to contact Little Rod, and inform him of his father's death. (Unsuccessfully . . . Little Rod wanders this earth, not knowing.) But one particular bundle of letters made me burn with curiosity—letters in another language.

I advertised, and found a student, or maybe it was a graduate student—at any rate a sniffy fellow named

Peter—to translate the letters. There were quite a few, and Peter charged me $500. He spent a lot of time on them, because the handwriting was so bad, he said, and the spelling was pretty shaky, too. He put them in Good English for me.

At first I was disappointed. I can't say precisely what I was looking for, some key to Uncle Rod—but whatever it was, it wasn't here. Pretty much run-of-the-mill love letters, like all the others, quickly sounding the same after the first few.

But one of the last letters stuck in my mind. I won't quote but a portion of it, but it spoke to me:

> *In your absence I take to my glass. But not always in loss, in sadness—sometimes I lift it to you, to us—to life. I have everything and nothing, nothing and everything, till it is empty.*

I don't care anymore what the rest of you think, or say about him. And that includes you, Aunt Pat, and you twins, and anybody else. Wagging tongues and bastards! These are my words now, without Rod. Let this testimony remain with you. I don't know where the dinosaur bone is: but I have only to look at the photo of the young corporal. Dear God. If he could see what's next. There is so much more to be.

Judith Gass-Curtis